The Best of Times

Walt Palmer

Sheaf Publishing   Sheffield

Dedicated to my precious grandchildren

First published in 1995 by Sheaf Publishing,
35 Mooroaks Road, Sheffield 10

ISBN 185048 017 6

Typeset in Bodoni and Clearface
Printed in Great Britain

Introduction

by Helen Jackson, MP for Sheffield Hillsborough

✳ ✳

WALT PALMER lives, as I do, in Grenoside, a village to the north-west of Sheffield. He was brought up – as I was – in industrial Yorkshire in the 1940s, and that time has left an indelible impression on him, which he now uses to create stories about a lovable and very funny gang of children growing up on the happy-hunting-ground of their own bombed-site.

During the early part of the Second World War, most towns were bombed to some extent, and the visiting aircraft left behind them ruined houses and works buildings which were cleared and then left neglected for years. In much the same way, twenty and thirty years later throughout industrial Yorkshire, first homes, then workplaces were once again arbitrarily demolished and the land on which they stood left idle.

Walt Palmer's gang had a bombed-site, a piece of land on which had once stood terraced houses and a church. It was theirs and theirs alone, by squatters' rights, a piece of territory on which to play and from which to watch the bewildering world around them, and the even more bewildering adults who inhabited it. Such places nowadays rarely exist, and where they do we would warn our children against them.

In the 1940s life for working-class children was simple and safe. When school ended you played out with your friends until supper-time, and in the summer you carried on afterwards until it got dark. During school holidays you could disappear for an afternoon or even a whole day, needing no more than a few sandwiches or the end of a loaf in your pocket, and – an occasional luxury – the bus or tram fare to some nearby woodland or open area. Some of us had bikes, and with my sandwiches in a basket the countryside was never far away, with minnows, grasshoppers, conkers, rose-hips and even – on one occasion – an angry bull in a field! We seemed in those days to walk miles and to have no worries. Cars were scarce, and apart from the well-known (but never specified) dangers of taking sweets from them, adults were not a real threat.

In those days before Tizer bottles and handy boxes of orange juice you would think nothing of knocking at an unknown adult's door and asking them for a drink of water. There *were* strange adults – every street probably had one – who rapped their front room windows if you made a noise, or went out and put hot ashes on your pavement slide in the winter, or even threatened to speak to your father about you, but in general adults were tolerated. Sometimes they even did things to help you or, best of all, slipped you some pocket money.

The simple, safe and uncomplicated world that I remember in my childhood is the one that Walt Palmer's gang inhabits. There was no television, so it was a world in which you created your own fantasies and learned the mysteries of life with and from friends of your own age. It was a place where you really believed you could invent mind-blowing schemes for making money or righting wrongs using only a frayed piece of string or something equally simple.

Above all, it was a place of comradeship and and childhood bonding and trust, where you learned each other's strengths and weaknesses. At times we were horribly cruel to each other and at others incredibly supportive, a process which helped 'knock the corners off', and at the end of each day everyone remained equal and ready for tomorrow.

In Walt's gang are children we will all recognise. Enoch is the leader, but astute Rosie is usually one step ahead of him, whilst Margaret, Brian, Herbert, Alan and Barry all play their part in the gang's activities. Among the adults, too, are people that I am sure I remember, and parents who must have been related to the parents of friends of mine!

Walt Palmer claims that his children were casualties of the Second World War, and so they were, brought up without fathers, who were away at the War, and in a world where the shortages were fairly shared. Yet perhaps that was a source of their strength, for it made them resourceful and independent and allowed them a safe and undemanding world of their own.

Into that world Walt Palmer now invites you, and I can thoroughly recommend it!

Tales from Foreign Parts

* *

IT HAD TAKEN a lot of effort by the gang to gain admittance to the Lyric Cinema to see the film *The Corn is Green*. Their first obstacle had been finding the money. This was eventually solved by selling back to Mr. Chippinghouse, the corner-shop owner, his empty pop bottles which they had purloined from the shop's backyard store.

The second obstacle was the film's classification. It was an 'A'. Children had to be accompanied with parents. They overcame this by begging and cajoling couples who were queuing to adopt them for the brief period between the ticket box and the ticket tearer. And so, with various temporary parents, each one eventually entered the dark cinema and became lost in the valleys of Wales and the seats of the scented pit.

The film affected them all in different ways and pre-occupied their talk over the coming days.

'Didn't them miners sing lovely?' Margaret breathed, as the gang sat on their individual house-bricks on the bombed site.

'Yer,' Rosie said dreamily, 'They were almond-icing you know... Welsh pit singers always bring a breath of Spring to the valleys. Look you, boy-oh.' Rosie had fallen in love with the Welsh accent and practiced it incessantly, much to Enoch's annoyance.

'Why are you talking in that daft way?' he asked, 'You've never been near Wales. It sounds daft saying "Look you" every two minutes... You're British. You're not a Welsh person.'

'You're jealous, Enoch Thompson', Rosie answered, 'You're jealous cos you can't speak Welshified.'

'I can if I want to,' Enoch replied, 'I can talk any foreign language if I want to.'

'Go on then, talk... er ... er ... talk Eskimolian.'

'I don't want to', Enoch replied, 'I like my own talk best... Foreigner talk is rubbish. That's why they all break their necks to learn our language... It's so they can understand what's going off in this world... Why should we talk in their words... We're the cock of the world... If they want to find out what's going off, they'd better smarten up and learn our talk. My Dad sez that's the trouble with going abroad, it's full of foreigners. No wonder the world is in such a mess . . . Nobody knows what's going off half the time, only us.' All the gang, except Rosie and Alan nodded in agreement.

Alan spoke.'The French think of us as foreigners.'

Enoch looked at him incredulously. 'What? Us foreigners? That's daft. How can we be foreigners? We're British through and through . . . that's just like them French people. Just because *they're* foreign they want us to be as well. They know that being British is the best thing to be in this world of ours . . . They're jealous cos they can't live here on this septic isle of ours and hold interesting discussions all day like us. They're too busy wearing striped jerseys and pedalling bikes about to sit down and talk interesting things. No wonder they grow up without being able to speak British.'

'Well, I don't think this is interesting talk', Rosie said. 'All you're doing is pulling foreign people to pieces. I think it's boring talk. And it would hurt their feelings if they heard you.'

'No it wouldn't', Enoch shot back, 'They wouldn't understand what I said. See. I told you speaking British was dead handy.' Enoch stood bursting with pride at his faultless logic, whilst Rosie retired from the argument and wondered how Enoch had gained entry into the human race.

Margaret stopped pulling at the loose thread of wool which was fast undoing her Mother's patient knitting, compared her unequal arm lengths, and said quietly, 'Mr. Friez can talk British and he's a German.'

'See', Enoch said, looking at Rosie. 'See what I mean. He took the trouble to learn our talk and look how high up the tree of life he's got. If he hadn't bothered to learn British I bet he'd still be in Germany preaching in foreign to Germans. God would have had a right time trying to mek out his prayers. I mean, He must receive thousands of British prayers every day . . . stands to reason that if a foreign prayer went up he'd put it to one side and not bother. Oh yes, Mr. Friez knew that the quickest way to God was to learn British. I bet God smiles on him all right for meking his job easier.'

The gang nodded in silent support.

'None of us are proper British', Margaret blurted out and immediately regretted doing so.

Enoch spun to face her, not believing his ears. 'What? What did you say?'

'Well, we're not', Margaret faltered. Then gathering her self-confidence, said defiantly, 'Mr. Mitchell, our history teacher, sez we're a bastard nation.'

Enoch's eyes nearly sprang from his head. 'We're a what?'

'Bastard nation', Margaret mumbled and blushed.

All the gang sat bolt upright and stared at Margaret with open mouths as the forbidden word bounced around inside their heads.

'Well he did', Margaret said, 'And it doesn't mean what you think it means.'

'Oh no?' Enoch sneered, 'Then what does it mean?'

'It means that we all came from different countries and races and settled here.'

'That's barmy', Enoch retorted, 'I was borned here. So were we all. Even our Dads were borned here. That Mr. Mitchell had better watch it. If my Dad gets to know he's been called a . . . a . . . you know what, he'll be down to school and give Mr. Mitchell a right leathering.'

'Yes. Mine as well', said Herbert.

'And mine', Brian and Alan chorused.

'No. Wait,' Margaret said desperately, 'You don't understand. It doesn't mean what you think it means. It means that in years gone by, hundreds of years gone by, this country of ours was invaded by Vikings and Great Danes and Anglos and Saxons. They all came and fought the proper Britons and they won.'

'Who were these proper Britons then?' Enoch sneered.

Margaret looked apprehensively at Rosie, took a deep breath, and said quietly, 'The Wales people.'

Rosie spun to face Margaret with menace in her eyes. 'That's right. Pick on the Wales people. Just because you're frightened of what you said,' Rosie spat out. 'Fancy picking on poor defenceless people like Wales singers who have never harmed anybody in the world . . . but once picked on will cause the sleeping lion to rise and Drake's Drum to beat a hasty retreat from where King Arthur is buried under the ground of Can-a-Lot with a sword of Dampy-Knees hanging over his head.'

'What the bloody 'eck does that mean?' asked a bewildered Enoch.

'It's hysterical talk . . . passed from father to son.'

'Well, how come you know it?' Enoch challenged, 'You're a girl.'

'I heard me Dad say something like it to me Mother once.'

'Oh,' Enoch said, with a puzzled expression on his face.

Rosie returned her stare to Margaret and said, 'So just you leave Wales singers alone in future . . . and pick on somebody your own size.'

Margaret felt hot tears well into her eyes, but fought them back and decided to keep a low profile for the present, yet Enoch pursued the topic. 'So what you're telling us, Margaret, is that we invaded this country and beat the Wales people.'

Margaret nodded her head ever so slightly.

'Hah, ha', Enoch said in triumph, 'So we are conquering heroes really, aren't we? We beat the Wales people . . . I bet really, we were the true Britons after all . . . I bet we'd only been away fighting foreigners and when we came back we found Wales people singing about all over our country and valleys, so we kicked them out again and told them to stick to singing in their pits and keep us supplied wiv coal.'

This statement sat easy on the gang's shoulders and so they accepted it as the truth. It felt better than being a load of bastards without a homeland.

Some time later, a roll of thunder sounded in the far distance. 'God's playing wiv his marbles again,' Alan said matter-of-factly, and glanced to where Barry was having a spitting contest with Herbert.

'I wonder if he's winning?' Brian asked.

'Don't know,' Alan replied and lobbed a piece of slate at the local one-eyed ginger tom cat. He missed. The cat paused, turned its head slowly, muttered an obscene word to itself, and sidled away in search of an unattached female with which to sustain his ancient family tree.

The thunder drew nearer. From doorways, pinafored women appeared like greyhounds from their traps. Soon, mouths were crammed with clothes pegs as line-hung washing was quickly rushed indoors to continue drying in front of polished Yorkshire ranges. The storm was approaching.

As the first heavy spots of rain began to pepper the bombed-site, the last of the gang entered their emergency den under the flat part of the bombed church. Alan lit the stub of candle which was always kept in the den for such occasions and they sat listening to the storm raging outside.

Suddenly Enoch jumped to his feet and, waving his fist at the den roof, yelled, 'O blow thy winter wind . . . blow with all thy mightiness. Sweep clean this flavoured land of ours.'

'Oh, no', Brian groaned, 'He's not starting again, is he?'

Rosie sniffed and said, 'The sooner they lock him away, the better.'

Alan nodded in support of Rosie. Enoch turned to face them.

'What do you mean, lock me away? That's poetry is that . . . It comes from the world famous pen of the Bard of all England . . . Billy Waggle Dagger.'

'If you mean William Shakespeare, say so. Calling him Billy Waggle Dagger is an insult to his memory', Rosie retorted.

'The trouble wiv you is that you're too touchy,' Enoch sniffed, and then, without invitation, launched into song.

'Land of rope and cory, Brothers of the flea,
How can we ex-store thee, Who were borned of thee,
Whiter still and whiter, Shall the pound be stretched,
Cod that made us mighty, mek us mightier yet.
Cod that made us mighty, mek us mightier yet.'

'Shakespeare's pen wrote that as well,' he announced proudly, 'It's called the Natural Hand-Thumb.'

4

'I like John Maize-Field best', Margaret spoke, 'I like his Highwayman poem . . . you know. The one about the moon and the purple moor, and that pub where Bess the Landlord's black-eyed daughter lives.'

'I bet he's a rough un,' Herbert remarked.

'Who?' Margaret questioned.

'The landlord of that moonlit pub. I mean, if he's always blacking his daughter's eyes, there's no telling what he'll do when a highwayman shows up for a fag and a pint.'

'I suppose you're right . . . I hadn't thought of that,' Margaret said.

A mighty roll of thunder rocked the ruins and a gust of wind found the candle flame. It spluttered then recovered. Enoch threw his head back, closed his eyes, and howled at the roof.

A shiver ran down Margaret's back.

'That was an Nound of the Basket Village, written by Shirelock Nomes', Enoch said, 'I read all the good books.'

'Have you read The Three Musket-Tears?' Barry asked.

'Yer . . . It's great isn't it?' Enoch replied and fenced his way around the den.

'Have you read Huckle Berries Fin?' Barry asked again.

'Yer. That's another great book. Especially that lad that's in it . . . er . . . Tom Sawyer. He gets up to some smashing adventures, doesn't he?'

'What about, er, Robinson Crusoe. Did yer like that?' Barry continued.

'Wow. Robinson Crusoe . . . I'll say . . . Now there is a great book. I've read it hundreds of times,' Enoch replied with enthusiasm.

'Are you sure you've read them all?' Barry quizzed.

'Yer,' Enoch said forcefully, 'Every one . . . I read all the great British books. That's what meks our country great . . . good reading books.'

'I agree wiv you,' Barry said. 'But it's funny, isn't it?'

'What is?'

There was a terrific flash of lightning followed by an ear-splitting roll of thunder.

Above the noise Barry shouted, 'All them books were written by foreigners.'

Drum Roll

* *

BRIAN STOOD caressing Enoch's drum whilst Enoch pretended nonchalant disinterest in his newly acquired possesion. 'It's smashing, isn't it?' Brian breathed.

'I suppose it's OK,' Enoch answered.

'OK? OK?' Brian exclaimed, 'It's the best drum I've ever seen. Can I have a bang?'

Enoch thought for some seconds then said generously, 'Yer, of course you can.' Then, as an after-thought added, 'Just one, though. I don't want it wearing out even before I've banged it on Sunday at the end of church parade.'

'Thanks, Enoch. Thanks a lot,' Brian gushed and made to take hold of the shiny new boy scout side-drum.

'Just a minute,' Enoch protested, 'I didn't say anything about holding it to bash it. I'll hold it. You bang it. And remember, just the one.'

'What shall I bash it with?' Brian enquired.

'Er,' Enoch said, looking around, 'Er . . . use that stick that's in the gutter.' Brian bent and retrieved the piece of rough wood which had drifted on the evening tide of the recent storm and was now left high and dry poking up between the bars of the street drain.

'Can I give it a big bash or just a little bash?' Brian enquired.

Enoch, who was in a generous mood, replied bigheartedly, 'You can have a special big bash. My drum can take it Brian. It was made by the best drum maker in all the world at large of ours.' He thrust his hip, on which the drum was slung, towards Brian and said, 'Bash away, Brian.'

Brian arced his arm high above his head, took a deep breath, and realising he was granted only one bang, determined to put every ounce of his strength into it. The hand-held stick descended in a quick blur of action. There was a tight staccato bang which was merged with a tearing sound and they both watched in horror as the taut skin split and hung loosely down into the drum shell. It was then that Enoch noticed the rusty nail which was sticking from the makeshift drumstick.

'Bloody 'eck,' they both hissed, 'That's torn it.'

'My new second-hand drum. Duff. And never played. What can I tell old

Wobbles?' Enoch whispered, referring to the Scout-master, who sported a large beer belly.

'Don't know,' Brian trembled.

'He's bound to take it off me now,' Enoch said moanfully, 'And I haven't even played it. I never have any luck. Not like other people who are in the lap of the gods.'

'Sorry,' Brian offered, 'But I didn't know there was a nail in the wood, did I?'

'Suppose not,' Enoch grunted, 'But what am I going to do now?'

'Don't know,' Brian said, helpfully.

Rosie crossed from the bombed-site, spotted Enoch and Brian, and joined them under the gas-lamp which was below Alan's bedroom window.

'Hello,' she greeted them cheerfully.

''Ello,' they answered miserably.

'Ooow, Enoch, your drum is bust,' Rosie exclaimed.

'I know,' Enoch replied.

'You can't bash a bust drum you know, Enoch,' Rosie continued.

'I know.'

'Well,' she sniffed, 'Seems daft to me carrying a bust drum about. Or are you just showing off?'

Enoch spun to face a smirking Rosie and snarled, 'No. I'm not showing off. He bust it just now. Didn't you, Brian?' Brian nodded.

'Why?' Rosie asked.

'Why what?'

'Why did you let Brian bust your drum?'

'I didn't let him bust it. He bust it accidentally with that stick.'

'You're supposed to bash drums with proper drumsticks not pieces of mouldy old wood with nails in them,' Rosie informed the two.

'We know that,' Brian snapped, 'But Enoch hasn't got proper drumsticks yet.'

'Not much point in having a drum without drumsticks. And if you did have proper drumsticks they would be no good now, would they?' Rosie remarked, 'Not with a noiseless drum to bash.'

'He could play the quiet bits,' Brian offered.

'Quiet bits?' Rosie laughed, 'They'd be deathly silent bits, if you ask me.'

'He'd be good at funerals, though,' Brian answered, 'He'd be the most popular drummer there. Banging his silent drum at the graveside when they were throwing muck onto their near-nest departed.'

'And,' Rosie supported, 'He'd be good at beating the midnight tattoo, wouldn't he? Those who were in bed would be dead grateful not to have their slumbering sweet dreams disturbed as he walked about thumping his silent drum.'

'Look, you two,' Enoch exploded, 'How much longer are you going to rabbit on? I want ideas for repairing my drum, not finding me other jobs to do.'

'You could stick it,' Rosie offered.

'Stick it? Stick it?' Enoch cried. 'How can I stick it? The pieces don't even meet now. Look.' He reached into the shell and demonstrated the gap between each ragged tear of the over-stretched skin.

'I see what you mean,' Brian said.

'I don't know about sticking the drum. It's me that's stuck,' Enoch moaned.

'Turn it over,' a voice sounded from above. They looked up and saw Alan looking down at them from his open bedroom window.

'What?' Rosie shouted.

'Turn it over,' Alan answered, 'It's got two sides. Bash the other.'

'Wow. What a brilliant idea,' Brian exclaimed.

'I can't bash an upside-down drum,' Enoch sneered, then added with an unsure note in his voice, 'Can I ?'

'Of course you can. It sounds the same whichever side you thump. Try it.' They watched as Enoch unclipped the side drum and, turning it over, sat it on the pavement.

'Go on. Hit it. Hit it,' Alan urged.

Enoch tentatively tapped the drum with his knuckles. A satisfactory thump, thump, sounded. He looked up at the three gang members and a great beaming smile split his face. 'It works,' he exclaimed, 'It works. I'm saved.'

'See,' Alan called, 'If you lot had got brains like what I have, you'd have deducted that solution without no effortness at all.'

'Eh?' Brian asked in a puzzled voice. Alan ignored him and called, 'I'll be down in a minute. I've just got to finish collecting fluff from under my bed. It's Saturday, don't forget.'

*   *   *   *

All the gang sat in a crossed-legged circle around the smokey fire in their favourite hollow on the bombed-site. Their faces sported warpaint soot marks and Rosie had stuck into her matted hair a feather which she had purloined from one of Mrs. Brigham's protesting chickens. Enoch sat to one side and solemnly thumped his drum.

'How,' Alan said, holding his hand up and turning to Brian.

'How,' Brian said turning to Rosie.

'How,' Rosie intoned, turning to Barry.

'Me know how. When?' Barry answered and burst out laughing.

'If you don't play the game properly, you won't play,' Rosie menaced, then turned away, and looking at the others braves said, 'Do you know, that indian drum is making my indian blood boil to bursting with it's hypnotise-motical beat,'

'Ugh,' Alan answered and nodded his head. 'I agree with you, squaw Rosie. It is a warmongering beat. I could just do with fighting a couple of hundred white settlers.'

Enoch heard their comments and increased the beat. 'You can have a dance around if you want to, oh my braves,' he called. 'The exercise will do you no end of goodness and get your bodies in a fighting mood.'

Rosie stood and began prancing around the fire. 'She looks a right fairy,' Barry whispered to Alan. Rosie heard the comment and as she danced level with Barry her hand casually swung out and clipped his ear.

'Sorry,' she said, 'I was carried away with the occasion.' Barry yelped and held his stinging ear whilst Rosie danced onwards with a smirk on her face.

'That's enough dancing about, oh my braves,' Enoch called. 'It is now time to do a bit of killing and things.' So saying, he ceased punishing the war drum, stood, and crossed to the camp-fire. 'Have you all got your hatchets, haxes, and Tommy's hawk?'

'Yer. Ugh,' the gang chorused eagerly.

'Right then, braves of mine, let us go and ham-bush some waggons on a train, to show the white man who speaks with a fork in his tongue that he can't mess about with Big Chief Drum-thumper.'

'Ugh. Yer,' the braves all answered.

'The first brave to bring me six lumps of hair which they have scalped from a white man's nut will become a brother of mine with the same blood.'

'It's making me feel sick. All this talk of killing and lumps of hair and blood,' Margaret whimpered, 'Why can't we play hospital?'

'Because they don't bang drums in hospitals, barm-pot. Only Indians bash drums,' Enoch sneered, 'And anyway, if you wasn't a cissy girl you wouldn't feel sick over a bit of blood and hair.'

'Hair that's dripping with blood, don't forget,' Herbert added eagerly. 'Yes, and dead settlers with millions of arrows in them,' Barry said.

'And blood oozing out of the arrow holes,' Herbert again added.

'Yer. And people pegged out in the desert covered in honey and a million hants nibbling at them.'

'And blood. There would be bound to be a lot of blood with all them hants,' Herbert once more put in his remark.

'Oh yes, there would be buckets of blood.'

They all watched keenly as Margaret turned pale and then a yellowy green. 'I'm going home,' she whimpered and turning, fled from the laughing indian's camp. They watched her run towards the street, and as their laughter subsided Alan said with a groan, 'Oh no. It's bedtime. The gas-lamp man is coming.'

They looked and saw the one-armed pedal pusher as he made his rounds lighting the distant street lamps.

'We'll finish the game tomorrow. Shall we?' Enoch asked.

'Yes,' they answered with enthusiasm. He turned, picked up his drum, and followed the gang as they split up to go their individual, terraced-house wigwams.

*   *   *   *

The following day was Sunday. Enoch stood outside the church with his up-side down drum clipped to his waist. Rosie stood in her dishevelled brownie uniform with the obligatory loose leg of her navy blue knickers flapping in the cool morning air. Alan, in his haste to get ready, lolled on the low church wall with his jersey the wrong way round and his woggle stuck on his thumb. It was beginning to hurt. Brian had not bothered to dress for the occasion, apart from a perfunctory gesture, namely, his cub hat, which he wore at a rakish angle in imitation of his current hero, Humphrey Bogart.

Margaret, as ever, was immaculately turned out, with creases in all the right places and pleats which would have severed legs. She constantly gestured with her left arm as she talked animatedly, hoping someone would compliment her on the rows of badges which she had earned or cajoled. Herbert was the only one not sporting any official dress. He had only recently joined the cubs and his mother, knowing his grasshopper mind, wasn't risking hard-earned cash on cub's outfits until she was sure he was maturing in his outlook towards group behaviour. Herbert stood eyeing the motley crowd and suddenly wished he was in the sea cadets. Herbert's mother was very wise.

'Right, you lot. Let's have you in ranks of three. Drums at the front. Trumpets behind them, and the banner carriers behind them. Smart now. Hurry up.' The Scoutmaster, or Mr. Wobbles as he was known amongst the gang, hitched his voluminous khaki shorts up around his enormous beer belly, tightened the chin strap of his scout hat, coughed, and quietly breaking wind, strode to the head of the disorganised procession.

Mr. Friez, the German vicar, crossed to take his place. He was careful to keep well upwind and to one side of Mr. Wobbles. He turned and smiled a holy smile at the mayhem to his rear. Drums were being tested. Trumpets dropped. Cubs and brownies were forgetting their good deeds for the day, and were pushing and thumping each other for the best position in the parade. Saint Alban's weekly church parade was about to shatter the peace of lay-a-bed, night before, beer bursting, sleepy heads.

*   *   *   *

'Oh my God. Not that bloody lot,' Mr. Chippinghouse, the corner shopkeeper, moaned through his befuddled head. He turned over and pulled the blankets up around his ears, then lay listening as the bedlam grew. He visualised himself knelt by the window with his finger on the trigger of a bren gun, with in its sights the entire church parade. He shuddered in ecstasy then groaned as the bang, bang, bang, grew louder.

'Keep it down, lads,' Wobbles bawled over his shoulder, 'Mrs. Biggin's husband isn't very well.'

'Bugger him,' Enoch thought, 'Nobody's going to stop me banging my drum. Besides. The music will cheer him up and do him no end of good.' He laid into the throbbing drum skin with re-newed vigour.'

The glass containing Mr. Biggin's false teeth, with two missing, jiggled along the dressing table and shattered as it hit the bare boards of his sick room. He let out a whimpering cry, sank back into his damp pillow, gasped, and lay still. Mrs. Biggins looked at him and decided on boiled ham as against potted meat for the funeral tea.

As the parade passed on its merry way, with the ever-present smile of Mr. Friez leading it, cats ran for cover, sparrows deserted fledgling offspring, pot dogs shattered and door-step milk curdled. Saint Alban's church parade was in full swing and like an avalanche nothing could stop its progress. Beads of perspiration trickled down Enoch's hot neck as his arms worked like windmills. He was deliriously happy, and yet one tiny nagging problem kept nipping at his thoughts. The broken drum skin. When old Wobbles discovered it he'd be out of the band forever.

'Keep in step, lads,' Wobbles called over his shoulder.

Around the corner of the street came Mr. Billy Burnco, the coal merchant. He crashed the gears of his ancient coal lorry, fought with the unco-operative steering wheel, straightened it, caught sight of the parade, cursed, and determined to drive straight up the highway. 'The buggers can get out of the way, I'm not,' he muttered.

The lorry and the parade were on a collision course. 'Don't worry, parade,' Mr. Wobbles called, 'Wheels give way to processions. March straight.'

Mr. Friez glanced apprehensively at the Scoutmaster and under the voluminous sleeve of his surplice he crossed his fingers. 'I'm sure it's steam gives way to sail,' he thought.

The lorry drew nearer, it's horn blaring, the driver more determined than ever to steer a straight course. Mr. Friez threw himself to one side as the mudguards reared high in front of him. Wobbles stood with wide eyes as the radiator grew to enormous proportions, then, deciding that discretion was the better part of valour, he flung his bulk onto the pavement shouting, 'Scatter, kids. The man's a maniac.'

The parade crumbled as neighbourhood offspring ran from the path of the lorry. Enoch stumbled on the shiny road. The weak clip holding his drum snapped, and as he sat on the refuge of the pavement the parade watched it rumble over the cobbles until it met the off-side wheel of the lorry. There was a splintering sound and the drum was shattered. They all watched with open mouths as the lorry crested the slope, turned the corner, and disappeared in a cloud of blue exhaust fumes. A stunned silence hung over the parade. Slowly Mr. Wobbles stood and crossed to Enoch who sat staring at the scattered pieces of the drum. A great weight was lifted from his mind. The evidence of the bust drum skin was gone.

'Never mind, son,' the Scoutmaster said as he patted Enoch. 'There's a brand new spare drum in the vestry. Cheer up.'

Enoch's heart leapt skywards. A cheeky, broad grin lit his face, and he asked thoughtfully, 'Does it have spare skins?'

Mr. Wobbles nodded kindly. Enoch sighed a contented sigh.

The vote collector

‘**W**HAT'S he doing?’ Barry asked as the gang watched a grey-suited man, sporting a red rosette on his lapel, proceed down the street knocking on doors and holding animated conversations with the door-stepped occupants.

‘He's begging.’ Enoch sniffed, as he fought to free the tangled string of his one-sided yo-yo.

‘He looks pretty well-off to be begging for a living.’ Herbert remarked.

Alan agreed, ‘Look at his posh suit. He can't be poor. The trousers match the jacket.’

‘And he hasn't any holes in his socks,’ Margaret observed. ‘I can't see him copping anything around here. He looks tons better off than this streetful.’

‘He's not begging for things,’ Enoch replied vaguely as he scowled at a stubborn knot.

‘Well, what's he begging for, then?’ Rosie demanded.

‘Votes.’

‘Votes?’ Alan queried, ‘Votes? What's them?’

‘It's what people give him, if they like him.’

‘Well, I've never seen any votes. We haven't got any. Not at our house. He'll be wasting his time if he knocks on our door,’ Rosie remarked.

‘No he won't,’ Enoch replied, ‘Your mum and dad have got one each. They'll give him one if they like him.’

‘How do you know what my mum and dad have got? You're lying.’

‘No, I'm not. Everyone gets a vote when they grow up.’

‘Who gives them these votes, then?’ Barry asked.

‘The government.’ Enoch said, matter of factly.

‘What can you do with them?’ Herbert wanted to know.

‘Give them back to the government,’ Enoch informed him.

‘That's daft is that,’ Rosie exclaimed, ‘What's the use of receiving something if all you do is give it back? They can't be worth much, these votes. Not if the government gives them away and the very people they give them to send them back.’

‘They're the most important things you can have in your life, my dad says,’

Enoch answered, 'Long, long ago, people used to fight and die just to try and get their hands on one of them. But now, the government 'as collected all the votes together and they give everybody one apiece for the rest of your natural borned lives.'

'Where's mine then?' Barry objected, 'How come everybody has one except me?'

'I haven't got one either,' Herbert complained.

'The government only gives them to grown-ups,' Enoch informed them.

'Typical,' Alan sniffed. 'The grown-ups always cop free things. I mean, haven't they got enough free things, what with . . . er . . . glasses, teeth, pills, and false legs. Now look. They even get a free vote. It's not fair, is it?' The rest of the gang shook their heads .

'Why is he wearing that red badge?' Margaret directed her question at yo-yoing Enoch.

'It shows which party he belongs to,' Enoch replied.

'Party? Party? They have free parties as well? Blimey. No wonder grown-ups keep telling us we should be seen and not heard. They want to keep all the scoff for themselves. Parties. Huh.' Brian exclaimed in disgust.

'No. No. You've got it wrong Brian,' Enoch said, slipping his yo-yo into his trouser pocket and joining the gang in the hollow on the bombed-site. 'Not parties, as in grub and pop. The party he belongs to is called the Labour Party. That's why he wears a red rosette.'

'Why?' Herbert stopped scratching his knee and asked.

'Because red is the colour of their party,' Enoch explained, 'The other party wears blue. That's the colour of their party.'

'Why?' Herbert persisted.

'Why what?' Enoch said with a slight edge to his voice.

'Why red and blue? Why do they wear colours?'

'So that people with votes to give away know they are giving them to the right bloke.'

'Who is the right bloke?' Barry queried.

'Whoever the people take a fancy to.'

'What happens then?' Rosie asked.

'Well,' Enoch replied, 'Whichever bloke gets the most votes, he wins.'

What?' Rosie persisted. 'What does he win?'

'Votes,' Enoch explained.

'What happens then?' Herbert asked.

'Well, my dad says he cops a bloody good job wearing his best suit all day in London.'

14

'Just for getting votes?' Margaret asked incredulously.

Enoch nodded his head wisely.

'It's a wonder all the grown-ups aren't at it, cadging votes from each other if that's the sort of rewards there are at the end of it.' Alan said.

'It's not as easy as that,' Enoch informed him, 'The reds and the blues are always at it, fighting each other for more votes. Sometimes the reds have the most. Sometimes the blues. And so it goes on.'

'What's it all for, though?' Brian queried.

'Search me,' Enoch answered.

'It's all very confusing isn't it?' Margaret spoke, 'Why can't the reds and blues share their votes equally? That would stop them fighting each other. I mean. It must cost them a fortune in best suits if they are always scrapping.'

'They can't do that,' Enoch said heavily, 'That would be betraying their party. No. It was agreed long ago in the mistiness of times gone by that the reds and blues would always fight each other for votes. And so it goes on.'

'Well I've never seen them having a punch up.' Alan said with a hint of disbelief.

'No. And you won't. Not around here, anyway,' Enoch replied.

'Why?' Brian asked.

'Because they don't do it around here. They go to a special place in London to do their fighting. It's called the house which is common. That's where they bash each other's brain boxes out for a living.'

Margaret spoke. 'My mum says only common people fight.'

'See?' Enoch said, 'See? That's why they go to this common house in London. They're ashamed of fighting in public and showing themselves up. That's why they go a long way from home to fight. It's so their neighbours won't get to know about their shameful habit of fighting all along. Oh yes. There are some right bloodbaths going on in that common house alright.'

'All that, just to collect more votes than everyone else. Shocking.' Brian said quietly.

'Too true, Brian. In fact, double double shocking.' Alan agreed.

'I bet if the King got to know what's going off in the midst of his fair capital he'd put his foot down with a firm hand and chuck them all in the Bloody Tower. Someone ought to tell him what's going on under 'is royal nose. Fighting on his very own donkey-stoned doorstep. It's disgustable, is that.' Herbert fumed.

'No. No. You've got it wrong,' Enoch said good-naturedly. 'The King knows all about it. Why, he even helps them.'

'How?' Rosie asked in disbelief.

'It's our King who goes along to the common house and opens it up for them.

After they've mopped the blood up from the previous punch-up, of course, and put fresh sawdust down. Oh no. The King likes to see them at it. I bet he has many a chuckle when he's sat on the throne listening to them.'

'Well, someone ought to put a stop to it,' Rosie said firmly. 'It could lead us innocent children into bad habits or something.'

'Yes. But who?' Margaret agreed.

The gang lapsed into silence until Enoch said thoughtfully, 'Miss Fillibut, the history teacher, says we are this country's future.'

'So what?' Brian asked.

'Well, I was thinking. Why don't we put a stop to it?' Enoch replied.

'How?' Alan looked up and asked.

Enoch pondered the question, then suddenly beamed and exclaimed, 'I've got it.'

'Is it catching?' Rosie smirked.

Enoch ignored her and gushed out his solution. 'The answer has been staring us in the face. I'll become a vote collector. I mean, there's no law against asking people for their votes, is there? I'll go from door to door and cadge them.'

'Which party will you belong to?' Herbert asked. 'Both.' Enoch announced, 'I'll wear half a red rosette and half a blue one. That way I'm bound to get everybody's vote. There will be no stopping me. It can't fail. It's brilliant. I mean. I can't fight myself, can I?'

'Wow,' Alan enthused, 'What a brilliant idea, Enoch. There's no doubt about it, when God handed out brain boxes he gave you a big one.'

'Yes,' Rosie muttered under her breath, 'But it's a pity it's empty.'

Enoch handed out his first political punch of his new career.

*　　*　　*　　*

'You see, Mrs. Biggins,' Enoch stood on her backyard doorstep and shouted, 'If you give me your vote I'll stop them fighting in that common house. I mean to say, there's too much of it going on, isn't there?'

'Eh?' Mrs. Biggins shouted above the howling of her hearing aid.

'And I'll see that you get a new deaf box,' he continued.

'Who's fighting?' Mrs. Biggins asked as she fought to untangle the electric wire from around her throat.

'They're all at it, Mrs. Biggins. Going at it like hammer and tongs. It's a disgrace.' The ear-piece plopped out onto her pinafored shoulder.

'Just a minute, love,' she panted, 'The damned thing's slipped out again.'

'Why don't you put some elastoplast over it?' Enoch bawled helpfully. 'Stick it in, like.'

'Hold on, love,' Mrs. Biggins gasped as the front of the battery box sprung open, spilling two corroded batteries onto her scrubbed flagstones. Enoch suppressed a sigh, bent, retrieved them for her, then watched as she fitted them back inside the rusting box. There was a small bright flash followed by a high-pitched whine which faded. A puff of blue smoke curled up from her ear. 'Well, that's buggered that,' she sighed. 'Bloody cheap thing. They don't make things to last these days, do they love?' Enoch shook his head in agreement.

'No. Everything's cheap and nasty,' she continued. 'And here's me thinking it would last me into my coffin.'

For a moment Enoch wondered why Mrs. Biggins wanted to be buried wearing her hearing aid. He didn't have time to dwell on the mystery, for suddenly she bawled, 'Randolph. Put it away, you dirty little bugger. It'll drop off and the dog will eat it.'

Enoch sighed, realised he was effectively cut off from communicating with Mrs. Biggins. Adjusting his mouldy piece of floorboard, to which was drawing-pinned two sheets of paper headed *People who have given me their votes*, he turned and retraced his steps up the entry.

He met with scant success at Mr. Lindley's after expounding his theories as to what he would do to the 'Trodden down on poor and ignorant hoy-po-loy who infested this septic isle', and when he offered his undying help in all matters, and had been dispatched to place a slip-bet with the illegal bookies runner at the corner of the street, he began to realise that getting votes from people was much harder than his simple plan had allowed for. In short, Enoch's political ambitions were suffering a severe attack of mid-term blues. And he'd not even had the opportunity of a good punch-up yet.

Three o'clock that afternoon, after a sudden heavy summer downpour, found a very disillusioned Enoch sitting on the pavement edge with downcast eyes, watching rain water gurgling along the gutter to the distant drain. A matchstick passed by, followed by a cigarette end, and a leaf which had decided to call it a day and get on with the business of Autumn. He sighed.

'Hello, Enoch.' A voice sounded behind him.

'Hello, Rosie,' he answered without looking up.

'How many votes have you cadged?' Rosie asked brightly.

'None.' Enoch replied quietly.

'Never mind,' she sympathised as she sat by his side, 'I'll tell you what. You can have mine when I grow up.'

'Thanks.' Enoch answered without enthusiasm.

'And I'm sure Alan, Herbert, Margaret, Brian, and Barry will give you theirs.'

Enoch lifted his head and looked at her. 'Do you think so?' he asked with a spark of hope.

'Yes,' Rosie replied confidently, 'Of course they will. After all, we're all in the same gang, aren't we? We've all taken the secret vow. Haven't we?'

'Yes. That's right,' Enoch breathed, 'We have, haven't we?'

Rosie smiled and nodded. 'Besides,' she went on, 'Our votes will be for keeps. Not like grown-ups. They're always changing their minds, aren't they? No. You can have all our votes for life. Through thickness and thin. We'll never ask for them back.'

'Thanks, Rosie. Thanks.' Enoch's face broke into a sunshine smile.

'So come on. Cheer up. Look, the sun's coming out. Lets go to our den and join the others.' They jumped up and ran happily across the steaming cobble-stones towards the bombed-site. A breeze pulled at Enoch's discarded, makeshift clipboard. The blank sheets tore free and caught in the gutter, then, riding the gurgling water, they sailed away and slipped from his life down the distant drain.

The Dodo's Dangler

• •

THE GANG sat in a line, with their knees drawn up to their chins and listened as, from the other side of the alley wall, Mrs. Brigham and Mrs. Lindley talked in a strange code about Mr. Bracewell, the local insurance man.

'My Albert says there is more than one way to skin a rabbit. He's going to let sleeping dogs lie for a bit, then set a sprat to catch a mackerel. That should cook his goose alright. My Albert is a wise old owl. He's got good horse-sense, has my Albert,' Mrs. Lindley informed her fellow conspirator.

'I quite agree,' Mrs. Brigham replied, 'It's about time he got his come-uppance. Mind you, he's as crafty as a cart load of monkeys. A right slippery eel if you ask me. Walking about like a cat that's got the cream.'

'Oh yes,' Mrs. Lindley went on, 'I used to think my Albert's bark was worse than his bite, but I've learned otherwise. He'll not rest until he catches him at it. Then he'll be at him like a bat out of hell. That will make my Albert as happy as a skylark.'

'Quite right too,' Mrs. Brigham supported, 'You needn't say any more. I quite understand. A nod's as good as a wink to a blind horse.'

'Well, I must be going now,' Mrs. Lindley sighed, lifting her shopping basket from the ground, 'I've got my Albert's tea to cook. He's like a bear with a sore head if he doesn't get it on time.'

'Aren't they all the same?' Mrs. Brigham replied, 'My Jack's just the same. Regular as a Dodo's dangler. Bye.'

Mrs. Lindley stood with a puzzled expression on her face at the parting remark. Finally she shrugged her shoulders then turned and walked down the alley.

'Who was that?' Alan asked as Brian climbed down from a pile of house-bricks which he had used to peer over the wall.

'Mrs. Brigham and old Mrs. Lindley,' Brian answered.

'Sounded like a passing circus to me,' Enoch sniffed, 'I don't think I'll ever understand grown-up talk.'

'What's a Dodo's dangler?' Rosie piped up.

'Search me,' Herbert said.

'Why? Have you got one hidden in your pocket?' Barry chuckled.

Herbert quickly reached and snapped Barry's rubber garter. 'Ow,' Barry yelled then glared.

'I wonder why a cart-load of monkeys are crafty?' Margaret puzzled.

'Don't know,' Enoch said. 'I suppose we'll never know until we grow up.'

'Suppose not,' Margaret agreed.

'Wow. Look at this,' Brian exclaimed. 'Wow. This is most interesting.'

'What is?' Enoch asked as the gang crowded around Brian. 'This brick. Look,' he said excitedly and pointed.

'What about it?'

'It's travelled all the way from London. Look. Look at the name on it. The London Brick Company.'

'So what?' Barry sneered.

'So what?' Brian exclaimed, 'It's travelled a lot further than any of us lot have ever travelled. It's a well-travelled brick, is that. I bet if it could talk it would have an interesting tale to tell.'

'Bricks haven't got mouths,' Rosie informed Brian.

'Perhaps not,' Brian conceded, 'But they make good listeners.'

'What do you mean, good listeners?' Enoch asked.

'Well, you know. Er, they must be good listeners. I heard Mr. Bracewell, the insurance man, telling Mr. Lindley's sister to be quiet when they were squeezing each other down the alley the other night. When she giggled he said 'Sshh. Walls have ears. They might hear us.'

'Oh,' the gang said in puzzlement.

'Fancy bricks having ears. I never knew that,' Alan said in hushed surprise. 'It just shows, doesn't it?'

'What's it show?' Enoch demanded.

'Don't know,' Alan replied, 'But it must show something.'

'There are more things in earth and heaven than are dreamed of by us mortals in the scheme of life's things. Horatio,' Rosie announced.

'Who said that?' Alan asked.

'She just did,' Enoch informed him.

'No. I mean who said it first?'

'Billy Waddle Dagger,' Herbert said blandly. 'He was always saying hard things to remember. I can't make tail or head of him. Especially that one where that woman is cleaning her upstairs windows and that man in a short skirt keeps shouting, "Juliet. Juliet. Chuck me a rose down." I mean, roses don't grow on window sills, do they? They grow in the garden where he's standing. And she must be daft. Shouting, "Romeo. Romeo. Where are you Romeo?" I mean, he's stood underneath her window, and she can't see him? She must be as blind as that horse that Mrs. Brigham was nodding and winking at.'

'Yes,' the gang supported.

'I don't know,' Barry sighed, 'Why can't people talk in ordinary plain English, like what me does. If everyone talked the King's English it would be a lot easier to understand. Wouldn't it?'

'Our King stutters,' Enoch informed Barry, 'That's hardly plain English, is it.'

'Well, no,' Barry conceded, 'But I mean, everybody's bound to have a stutterer or a limper in their famberly sooner or later, aren't they? It's up to us to help them over their hurdles to a brighter life, free of limping and stuttering.'

'Suppose so,' Enoch agreed reluctantly, 'But what I was trying to say was, that if everybody spoke the King's English we'd be a country of stutterers, wouldn't we? That would cause no end of chaos, wouldn't it? It would take ever so long to read the news out on the radio, and they'd have to print newspapers full of stuttering words. It would take a fortnight or perhaps even longer, two weeks, just to read one paper, wouldn't it?' Barry nodded his head in silent agreement whilst Rosie's brain worked overtime, trying to find a flaw in Enoch's reasoning. She gave up.

'Oh no,' Enoch continued, 'The King's English is alright at times, but I'd rather talk like what I was taught to talk at my mother's knee-caps, back in the mistiness of time.'

'Yes,' Herbert piped up, 'I agree with you, Enoch. If Billy Waddle Dagger had talked plain English instead of all the 'where fors' and 'harkens', perhaps a lot more people would have bought his books. Why, if he'd talked good old plain English, I bet he'd be world-fainemous by now. It's talking backwards way round that has kept old Billy poor and unknown. Why didn't he stick to what his mother's knees taught him? That's what I can't understand. I mean. I bet he never heard his mother say, "Harken, William. I can hear your father where-to-foreing his way home for his evening meal". Did he? No. All she said was, "Billy, your dad's home from work." That's all.'

'Very true,' Enoch agreed wisely, 'You talk some very true things at times, Herbert.'

'At other times all he does is talk rubbish,' Rosie whispered to Margaret. Margaret giggled. Herbert glared.

'Why were they squeezing each other in the alley?' Barry suddenly asked.

'Who?' Herbert questioned.

'You know. Brian said Mr. Bracewell and Mr. Lindley's sister were whispering to the wall and squeezing each other. Why?'

'Oh that,' Herbert exclaimed. 'Why *were* they squeezing each other?' He turned and directed the question at Brian.

'It's something to do with being grown-up,' Brian answered, with an unsure tone in his voice. Then added, 'I think.'

'No doubt we'll learn about it when we're grown-up,' Enoch said.

'There's a lot of things we've still to get to know. I expect squeezing is one of them. I suppose it's a bit like tickling each other, but more grown-uppish.'

'I wish God had made our hands so that they could spin right round,' Alan called to the rest of them.

'Why?' Margaret enquired.

'Because I've got mine stuck in this flippin' tin can,' Alan gasped.

'That's a daft thing to have gone and done,' Rosie called.

'I didn't do it on purpose, burke,' Alan scowled, 'It was an accident. I thought I saw something very interesting at the bottom of the tin.'

'What was it?' Herbert asked.

'I don't know, do I?' Alan exclaimed, 'That's why I reached in to see what it was.'

'What's it feel like,' Enoch asked, with academic interest.

'Very tight,' Alan panted.

'No. Not the tin. I mean whatever it was you reached in for.'

'There's nothing in the tin. I made a mistake. It was my reflection looking back at me from the polished bottom.'

'I'm glad God didn't give us polished bottoms,' Brian smirked. 'Just imagine trying to sit down. Whoosh. Straight onto the floor. Chairs would be useless, wouldn't they, unless they were made with a little round hole in the seat.'

'Very true, Brian,' Enoch congratulated, 'You find some very interesting things to talk about. I bet when you grow up you'll become a great thinker, or something else.'

'Thanks, Enoch. Thanks,' Brian gushed.

'Can someone help me?' Alan called desperately.

The gang sauntered over to where Alan stood tugging at the imprisoning tin. Forming a circle around him, they watched with interest as Alan struggled and panted and cursed at the un-yielding metal.

'That's a right problem you're stuck with,' Herbert said thoughtfully.

'A most unusual problem,' Enoch agreed, 'I've seen tinned corned beef, tinned beans and tinned tomatoes. But do you know, that's the first time I've seen tinned hand.'

'Can't see it catching on, though,' Barry remarked.

'Oh, I don't know,' Brian answered, 'Cannibals would find it dead handy.' The gang chuckled whilst Alan continued sweating and struggling. Suddenly, with a painful yell, the tin shot free of his red hand and fell to the ground. Alan let out a sigh of relief then began massaging his sore wrist. One by one they returned to their places by the alley wall and sat in the warm sunshine.

'Ne'er cast a clout till May is out,' Margaret whispered sleepily.

'It's July,' Enoch answered through half-closed eyes.

'Oh 'eck,' Brian sighed, 'I've missed clout-casting time again. Now I will have to wait until next year before I can feel comfortable again.'

'Burke,' Margaret mumbled.

'It's very inconvenient, isn't it?' Herbert breathed and stretched.

'What is?' Rosie asked.

'Sweating,' Herbert replied, 'Sweating is very inconvenient. Leaking skin. Very inconvenient. I mean, you just get comfortable in the sunshine, then, whoosh, leaking skin all over the place.'

'Yes,' Barry agreed. 'Mind you. It's a lot hotter in deepest, darkest, African jungle. I bet they sweat a lot more than us.'

'Ah, yes. But don't forget this,' Enoch muttered lazily, 'In Africa the government lets the people walk about with no clothes on to keep cool. Not like our government. I mean if we walked about clothesless they'd have a blue fit, wouldn't they?'

'And no-one would be able to tell what anyone else did,' Herbert added.

'I mean. Imagine P.C. King arresting someone with no clothes on. Where would he keep his truncheon and whistle for a start?'

'The mind boggles,' Rosie mumbled.

'He could pull a little trolley with a box on it,' Brian offered, 'Just imagine. P.C. King walking his beat, clothesless, pulling his tackle.'

The gang began to giggle then collapsed with laughter at the bizarre picture Brian had painted. 'Imagine him in court,' Enoch spluttered, taking up the stance of P.C. Neville King. 'I was proceeding down the road, your honour, when I saw this bare burglar's bum climbing out of a window. Quick as a flash I withdrew my tackle from a box which I keep handy on my official trolley and without further ado, I accosted him.'

'How did you know he was a crinimal, P.C. King?' Brian joined the game as the judge.

'Well, your honourableness, he had striped skin.'

'Striped skin, P.C. King?'

'Yes, your worshipfulness. Striped skin. I expect he got it sunbathing behind bars.'

'Well done, P.C. King. I will see that you cop a medal for this brilliant piece of crime fighting.'

'Thank you, your judgeness,' Enoch bowed, then laughed anew. 'One without a pin on the back, though!'

The gang felt elated as the two sat down once more. Eventually they decided to visit their den on the bombed-site and crossed the scrubby grass by the local brickworks. As they approached the top of the road which led to the ruins they saw in the distance P.C. Neville King, pedalling his bicycle towards them. He drew level, and raising one hand in an official wave, he nodded his head in their direction. The gang respectfully waved back, then watched as he free-wheeled his way down the hill which led to the police station.

'My dad says crime around here 'as shot up since P.C. King became mobile,' Rosie announced, 'I mean, he spends all day whizzing past crime. He can't see much from a whizzing bicycle saddle, can he? My dad says crime was much less when he had to walk his beat.'

'You can't stop progress, Rosie,' Enoch said wisely, 'The police have got to move as fast as these times we live in.'

'Suppose so,' Rosie agreed sulkily.

'Oh yes,' Enoch went on, 'I bet it's not long before burglars get bikes and become mobile. I bet this is just the start of modern crime and bad things.' Suddenly there was a strangled cry to their rear. They all spun around and watched with interest as Mr. Lindley stood in the street and endeavoured to reduce the size of the neck of Mr. Bracewell, the insurance man, in his great hairy hands, shouting, 'I'll teach you to meddle with my sister.'

'See? See what I mean?' Rosie exclaimed, 'Crime all around and P.C. King miles away pedalling his bike.'

The gang wasn't listening. They were preoccupied with the insurance man's fight for survival. With a supreme effort born of desperation, he raised his heavy collecting book and brought it down on Mr. Lindley's head. Surprise showed for a fraction of a second, then his grip relaxed and Mr. Lindley crumpled to the ground. Without pausing to inspect the results of the blow, Mr. Bracewell grabbed his fallen bicycle, threw himself into the saddle, and pedalling furiously away down the street, vowed never again to collect Mr. Lindley's death money.

'Mr. Lindley doesn't look as happy as a skylark now, does he?' Brian said quietly.

'More like that bear with a sore head,' Alan said.

'He looks as dead as a Dodo's dangler to me,' Enoch sniffed.

The Forgetful Highwayman

Whenever the moon and stars are set,
Whenever the wind is high,
All night long in the cold and wet,
A man goes riding by.

ENOCH STOOD with his Dad's flat cap on his head, an old piece of lace curtain tied around his neck, and Alan's cap pistol stuffed down his trousers. He crossed to the door of the bombed house and tapped on it with a short piece of stick. A voice shouted from inside. 'Who's there?'

'Is your black-eyed daughter in, landlord?'

'Who wants to know?' Alan the landlord asked.

'It's me. The highwayman.'

'We're shut for the night. Go away.'

Enoch turned and crossed the building rubble until he stood under the bedroom window. He reached down, grasped half a house-brick and straightening, lobbed it at the window. It hit the one remaining pane of glass which shattered inwards. There was a muffled scream from inside and Rosie appeared at the casement.

'Who threw that bloody brick?' she shouted through bright red, liquorice torpedoed lips. Then stared down through eyes that were coated with soot at highwayman Enoch.

'It's me. The Highwayman,' Enoch hissed, 'Be quiet. You'll wake everybody up.'

'That's as may be,' Rosie exclaimed, 'But you're supposed to whistle a tune at my window, not chuck a brick through it. You could have killed somebody in here. Don't forget, my bedroom is full of soldiers with red coats on. It only just missed Brian. Now pack it in and whistle.'

'Sorry,' Enoch said, 'But I did say I'd come to thee by moonlight. But your Dad said you weren't in.'

'Oh, alright Highwayman. I'll forgive you. Now get on with it.' Enoch pursed his lips and emitted an ear-shattering whistle, then called, 'Bess. Bess, the landlord's black-eyed daughter. Are you in bed?'

Rosie appeared at the window again and looked down at Enoch seductively. He was running on the spot and smacking his behind with one hand. 'Woe. Woe', he called to his invisible horse.

'Oh, hello Highwayman,' she breathed.

'Hello', Enoch answered, 'I've just come over the purple moor. That road is just like a ribbon of moonlight. You can see for miles. Do you like my highwayman's outfit?'

Rosie nodded, then said, 'I've put some red ribbon in my hair for you. To show I love you. Do you like it?'

'Don't be sloppy,' Enoch answered.

From inside the bedroom there came a muffled yell.

'What was that?' the highwayman asked.

Rosie turned her head, then said, 'One of the soldiers has just fallen through the floorboards. I think it was Barry.'

'Oh,' Enoch said, 'It's dangerous living in these olden times isn't it? What with King George's men always marching about and all these condemned houses that are only fit for the poor.'

Rosie agreed, then asked, 'Have you seen Tim the Ostler anywhere? He's in love with me, you know, even though he's got mouldy hair. He gets dead jealous of highwaymen. I'd watch it if I was you.'

'Don't worry', Enoch said fearlessly, 'I've got a job on tonight. I'm after some gold. So I'm going to be busy. Chuck us your hair down, then I'll be off.'

From inside the bedroom came a crashing sound.

'What's that?' Enoch enquired.

Rosie looked once more. 'Herbert got his musket caught in the banister rail. He's just fallen downstairs.'

'Oh,' Enoch said, 'At this rate there will be no soldiers left to kill you.'

'I know,' Rosie answered, 'They've been larking about for ages up here. I'm fed up with them.'

'Well, I'll be off now. I'll see you tomorrow,' the highwayman informed black-eyed Bess.

From inside her boudoir a redcoat's voice enquired, 'As he gone yet?'

Rosie turned. 'No, he's just going now.'

'Good job. We want to tie you up to attention, with a musket under your breast.'

'That's a rude word, is that,' Enoch protested.

Brian appeared at the window. 'No it's not. It's in the poem, see. Now you clear off and don't come back until tomorrow. We've got work to do. We've got to tie Rosie, I mean Bess, by her foot to the bed. Then we've got to gag her, don't forget. At this rate we'll have no time to drink her Dad's ale without talking to him.'

'Right-o,' Enoch called, 'I'm off over the purple moor now. Ta-rah.' Enoch galloped across the bombed-site and was lost in the autumn smog which filtered from the steelworks.

Alan, who had swopped jobs and joined the army, helped Brian, Herbert and Barry in tying-up Rosie with an old piece of washing line. Secured between her and the rope was a short piece of floorboarding. 'Ooow. Not too tight', she protested, 'I'll never reach the trigger when my bonny sweetheart comes back.'

'Sorry,' Alan mumbled.

'We'd better take up our positions by the window,' Herbert said, 'so that we can ambush the highwayman.'

They all made to move to the window. 'Just a minute,' Rosie exclaimed, 'Haven't you lot forgotten something?'

'What?' Alan asked.

'You're supposed to have a sniggering jest at me. Then kiss me in turn.'

Alan stood for a moment looking at Rosie's smeared face, then said, 'Well, I don't mind doing a sniggering jest, but kissing is right out.'

The rest of the redcoats nodded in agreement. Rosie glared at them, her chance of a quick ravishing gone. She began to sulk.

'Right, men. Guard the window,' Alan commanded. They crossed to the casement and squashed together to peer out. There wasn't enough room for Brian and he complained. 'I can't see the road over the purple moor with you lot crowding the window.'

'We'll tell you when he's coming,' Alan hissed, 'Now shut up.'

Brian began to sulk and mutter to himself. 'It's not fair. I'm a redcoat as well. I never get a chance. It's always me that has to miss out. Every time. It's me. I'm fed up. It's alright for them, they can see out of the window. I can't. They can. It's always me.'

'Oh, shut up, you big mardy bum,' Herbert called.

Brian threw his musket at him. It missed and hit Barry.

'Right,' Barry exploded, and ran at Brian. In a flash all the redcoats were fighting on the bedroom floor, with a restrained Bess shouting encouragement to first one then the other.

'The winner can kiss me,' she yelled.

As if by magic, they all pulled apart. 'Who won?' Rosie asked eagerly.

'Nobody,' Alan said quickly, 'It was a draw.'

Rosie resumed her sulk. As the noise died down they heard a faint noise. 'Tlot. Tlot.'

'He's coming,' Barry exclaimed. They ran back to the window, with pounding hearts.

'Tlot. Tlot.'

'Oh yes, men, he's on his way back alright,' Alan said, 'We'd better look to our priming.' The gang pretended to load their muskets.

'Tlot. Tlot.'

Suddenly, from behind them, Rosie yelled. 'Bang. Bang.'

Brian jumped. 'Bloody 'eck. What was that?'

'Rosie has shot herself like in the poem.'

'Is she dead?'

Rosie half lifted her drooping head and hissed, 'Of course I am. I've killed myself to warn my highwayman that you're all in my bedroom.'

'That's not fair,' Brian exclaimed, forgetting the poem and knowing only that he'd missed his chance to kill Enoch for once in his life.

'He'll be back,' Bess answered, 'If you'd read the poem you'd know that.'

'Oh,' Brian said, appeased that he would get another chance to shoot Enoch the highwayman.

Enoch heard Rosie kill herself and said in desperation, 'We'd better clear off, Black Beauty. Something's up at the inn. We'll come back tomorrow morning when it's quietened down a bit. Giddy-up.' He reined-in his trusty steed and galloped back into the thickening fog.

The redcoats now lay in wait on the bombed-site. Each one lay in shallow depressions which formed a large circle. The fog blanketed everything and visibility was down to only four feet.

'Is he here yet?' Barry hissed.

'Who's that?' Alan asked.

'Whose who?'

'It's me,' Herbert replied.

'Is he here yet?' Barry hissed again.

'Who?'

'The highwayman.'

'Who's asking?' Alan asked.

'It's me', Herbert replied.

'What? Barry asked.

'No. Not yet', Alan said.

'What?' Herbert asked.

'Is he here yet?'

Suddenly they heard, 'Tlot. Tlot', then a fall to the ground, followed by a curse. 'Flippin' 'eck. I can't see a thing. Tlot. Tlot. Ooow. Blinking house-bricks.'

'He's coming,' Alan hissed.

'What?' Herbert said.

'Is he here yet?' Barry asked.

'Who's that?' Brian enquired.

'What?' Herbert said.

'Tlot. Tlot.' There was a crash as Enoch the highwayman fell against a rusting dustbin. 'I think I'd better dismount and walk,' he mumbled, 'It's much safer.'

'Steady, men. He's nearly here now,' Alan breathed.

'What?' Herbert asked.

'Is he here yet?' Barry continued to enquire.

'Quiet. He will hear us.'

'What?'

'Is he here yet?'

'Who's that?' Enoch the highwayman hissed through the fog.

'What?'

'Is he here yet?'

'I don't know,' Enoch whispered. 'Who are you looking for?'

'Who's that?' Brian asked.

'It's me,' Alan answered.

'Is he here yet?' Barry said.

'I don't think so,' Enoch replied.

'We'd better get ready,' Alan informed them.

'Right.'

'What?'

'Is he here yet?'

'Tlot. Tlot.'

'Wow,' Alan whispered, 'He sounds quite near now. Steady, men. When you see him, shoot him down like a dog on the highway.'

'Right', Enoch hissed, 'Tlot. Tlot.'

'Is he here yet?' Barry enquired.

'I can't see him because of this fog. But I can hear his horse,' Brian said.

Suddenly the fog parted, leaving Enoch standing in the middle of the circle of redcoats. For some seconds they all stared at him. Then Alan shouted, 'Fire. Kill him.'

Muskets exploded and the highwayman dropped dramatically to the ground with his bunch of lace at his throat.

'Well, that's the end of him,' Brian said. 'So die all perishing robbers.'

Alan agreed. 'Shall we go to our den and light a fire?'

'Good idea,' Enoch said, rising from the dust, and together the redcoats and the highwayman melted into the fog.

'I'll kill them when I get free,' Rosie sobbed, 'They always forget me. It's not fair.' She lay on the dirty bedroom floor removing the last of the rope which had held her prisoner. Through the open window she could hear the muffled sounds of the gang laughing, away in the distance.

'I'm not going to play with them any more.' She bit her lip as hot tears began to flood her black eyes, and mixing with the soot, streaked her face.

'They never appreciate me. I'm going home to play with me doll.' She stood, and pulling at her hair threw the piece of red rag and her love for the highwayman through the open window. As she did so a line from the poem entered her head.

'I'll come to thee by moonlight, though hell should bar my way.'

Rosie's red lips pursed. Her eyes narrowed, and she thought, 'I'll give him hell when I see him tomorrow.'

Full Circle

* *

'WELL, I think she'll look a right mess', Enoch sneered, 'Fancy going into church carrying a bucket and dragging a train behind her. And another thing, why does she need a boy dressed up in paper? She'll be a right laughing sock around here.'

The gang had journeyed from their den on the bombed-site and now sat on a rotting log by the pit yard out-flow, discussing Rosie's auntie's forthcoming wedding to Tommy Taylor, the last eligible bachelor to inhabit the smoky environs of the street of terraced-houses. She had stalked him patiently over the years, plying him with home-made parkin, sheep's heads, and the occasional parcel of vinegared tripe, until, in a moment of weakness, and whilst the radio was playing *Moonlight Serenade* in her washing-hung kitchen, his eyes had been caught by her pink satin, no-nonsense gusseted cami-knickers dripping onto the pegged hearth-rug.

His blood had boiled, his sixty-two year old heart had opened, and through his toothless mouth, he had popped the question. Coyness wasn't Ida Bullivant's strong point after having spent thirty years behind the counter of the steelworks canteen, but she gave it a token gesture by turning her head away and saying, 'Oh Tommy. What a surprise.'

Then, not giving him chance to retract his proposal, and whilst his eyes feasted on her dripping, off-white 'D'-cup corset, she added hastily, 'Yes.'

They grappled clumsily and she accepted his stubbly kiss. It felt as though her mouth was pressed against a wet scrubbing brush. But she was distracted from the overt affection. Her mind was already on the more important matter of where he kept his insurance policies and Co-op dividend money.

'It's not a bucket. It's a bouquet', Rosie explained impatiently, 'And it isn't a boy covered in paper. It's a page-boy. They're lovely are page-boys. Every wedding has one.'

'I didn't see one at my mum's wedding', Brian said, 'I was sat right up front, and I didn't see no page-boy.'

'Your mother's wedding was different', Rosie answered, 'You were borned years before your dad came back from the war. I mean, it would have looked daft with you sat there and a page-boy at your mother's side.'

'Oh,' Brian said.

'Anyway,' Enoch persisted, 'What about the train?'

'It's not a real train, burke. It's just a name they give to that piece of cloth which hangs down her back,' Rosie exclaimed.

'Well, I don't know,' Enoch sighed, 'It seems very complicated does this wedding business. I mean, all that dressing up and things. Seems potty to me.'

'It's what every woman longs for,' Margaret said dreamily, 'A white wedding in the spring, with all the flowers out and the sun shining and the birds singing and the churchbells ringing and the choir singing and the . . . er, you know, loads of other things.'

'Seems sloppy to me,' Alan spoke, 'Trust girls to invent something daft for themselves like weddings. If it had been left to us men . . . '

'You aren't a man yet,' Rosie protested.

'No. Not yet. But I will be one day,' Alan conceded, then continued, 'If it had been left to men, there wouldn't be any sloppy bits or flowers and things. Waste of good money is that. Oh, no. It would be straight down the aisle, a quick yes, and then straight into the receptional for a good blow-out.'

'Yes,' the male members of the gang agreed.

'Typical,' Rosie sneered.

'I can't see why she wants to marry old Tommy Taylor, anyway,' Barry joined in, 'He must be a thousand years old if he's a day. Shouldn't be surprised if he doesn't make it to his day of the wedding. Not with his gammy legs and pot eye. My dad says he's got a right graveyard cough, as well.'

'I saw him take it out once,' Margaret spoke.

Enoch giggled.

'No. Not that,' Margaret scowled. 'Don't be rude. His eye. I meant his eye. He took it out, put it in his mouth, rolled it around, then put it back.'

'What for?' Brian asked.

'To clean it,' Margaret said blandly.

'If he'd have swallowed it, his eye would have been as big as his belly,' Enoch laughed.

'Why?' Barry asked in a puzzled voice.

Enoch shook his head and said, 'It doesn't matter, Barry. You wouldn't understand. It's a joke.'

'And a poor one at that,' Rosie sneered.

'When is the wedding?' Brian enquired.

'This weekend, I think,' Rosie answered, 'My mother says my auntie Ida wants to get him down the aisle quick before he pops his clogs.'

'That's good thinking,' Margaret said in praise.

'Oh yes,' Rosie continued, 'When my auntie Ida decides to do anything, she does it. No messing about. She'll have him down that aisle quick as a flash. His feet won't touch the ground. Whoosh. Bang. Married, and living happily ever after.'

'Poor old Tommy,' Enoch muttered, 'He doesn't stand a chance against a screaming woman. Someone ought to tell him about his coming doomness before its too late. Doomed he is forever. Doomed to sheep's heads, tripe and onions, parkin, and chitterlins and bag for the rest of his life.'

'What do you mean, doomed?' Rosie said indignantly, 'My auntie Ida will make him a good wife.'

'What will she use?' Alan giggled, 'A sheep's head and chitterlins?'

Rosie gave Alan a disgusted look then continued making her daisy chain from the dandelions which grew in the soggy ground.

'Are you going to the wedding, Rosie?' Margaret enquired as she passed a freshly picked flower to her.

'Oh yes,' Rosie enthused, 'I,' she emphasised the word, 'I am going to be a bridesmaid.'

'Uh,' Enoch scoffed, 'It'll look a right pig's ear. Glad I'm not going.'

'So am I,' Rosie said forcefully.

Suddenly a howling scream tore at the air. The gang shot to their feet and stared across the pit yard. Men were running from low buildings calling to each other. 'Wow,' Enoch breathed, 'That's the disaster siren. There's been an accident. Come on.'

The gang ran towards the pit gates then stood watching as a green ambulance rounded the time house and roared towards a high building which led to the shaft entrance. Clouds of coal dust billowed in its wake. From behind them the sound of a lorry's engine grew. They turned and watched it racing up the rough road towards the gates. As it drew level and thundered past, Alan shouted, 'It's the mines rescue lorry.'

Great plumes of pure white steam pulsed into the air from the engine house, and the twin winding wheels began to spin until they became a blur. Startled pigeons fluttered from their roosts and swooped down onto the bath house roof. 'Wow. It's exciting, isn't it?' Barry whispered, 'A real live pit disaster on our very own doorsteps.'

'It must be our lucky day,' Brian said, 'This will be something to tell our fore-fathers when we grow up.'

'You mean children, burke,' Rosie corrected.

'Them as well,' Brian answered.

'A real dramatic drama of a pit disaster. And we are lucky enough to be witnesses with our very own eyes,' Alan added.

'Just imagine,' Enoch exclaimed, 'Millions of toilers of the deep struggling at this very minute beneath our feet. Struggling to sing miners' songs to keep cheerful, and passing bottles of water around in a friendly gesture of miners' togetherness.'

'And lifting pit props off each other,' Brian joined in. 'I mean, there's bound to be lots of pit props, isn't there?'

'And men pushing through tiny holes to reach trapped young miners who are the sons of other miners and who have only gone down the pit because there is no other work, and left their mothers fiddling with the salt pot and crying at the kitchen table.'

'And there will be a lot of holding candles up to see which way the wind is blowing,' Herbert added. 'And old miners who knew all along that the roof was unsafe and warned the others when the rats left the tunnels but they took no notice and laughed at him,' Enoch continued.

'Yes,' the gang breathed.

'All that happening under our feet at this very moment in time. Wish I had X-ray eyes,' Brian said wistfully.

Suddenly the siren died and a deathly hush descended, broken only by the steady throb and belch of the mighty winding engines. The gang continued to stare towards the down shaft building, each one silently living a thousand heroic deeds of rescue, praise, and medals. From a door in the time-house, a bowler-hatted man strode into the centre of the yard. He hooked a pocket watch from his waistcoat pocket, glanced at it, raised a whistle to his mouth, and blew a long shrill note. Removing the whistle he shouted, 'Stand down. Practice over, lads.' The gang turned and looked at each other with puzzled expressions.

'It was a practice. Only a flippin' practice,' Enoch exclaimed. 'Flippin' 'eck. Just a flippin' practice. What a waste of time.'

Rosie stared at him in disbelief. 'You really wanted it to be real, didn't you?' she said, 'You really wanted a pit disaster on your hands. I don't believe you. You've no feelings at all. You're horrible.'

'Well,' Enoch mumbled in embarrassment, 'Well, no. No, I didn't.'

'Yes, you did. You're really disappointed, aren't you?'

'No I'm not,' Enoch defended, 'It's just that, er, well, er, you know. Oh, shut up. You're just a cissy girl. You don't understand. Does she?' Enoch turned to the others for support. The rest of the gang stood looking at their feet in an embarrassed silence. 'Does she Brian?' Enoch half pleaded.

Brian shook his head reluctantly.

'See,' Enoch said, then with gathering confidence went on, 'I knew it was a practice all along. I was just pretending. And you fell for it.' He laughed falsely to bolster his statement. 'Oh, come on. Let's go and play. I'm fed up with this pit yard anyway.'

Enoch set off down the rough road which was edged with stunted, dust covered bushes. Soon the pit was lost from view and in a short time the gang was its normal rowdy self, all thoughts of the experience forgotten.

*   *   *   *

Sometime later, as they sat in a line on the lichen-covered rickety fence which bordered Mr. Parker's rhubarb plantation, watching the old gardener patiently erecting a scarecrow to protect the great creamy seed heads, Alan observed, 'That scarecrow is wearing better clothes than Mr. Parker.'

'That's true,' Enoch agreed as he shielded his eyes against the hazy sun. 'Come to think of it, it's wearing better clothes than any of us.'

'Yes,' the gang agreed.

'I wonder why there are only men scarecrows?' Brian asked. 'I mean, you never see a woman scarecrow do you? Only men scarecrows. There must be a logi, er, lograth, er, good reason for that.'

Enoch pondered this for a while then announced, 'It's because it's a man's world, Brian. Men are the best looker-afterers of this world. Tons better than sloppy girls.'

Rosie and Margaret reacted immediately to this heretical statement as Enoch knew they would. 'Huh,' Rosie fumed, 'Man's world. Some man's world. If it wasn't for us women you lot would starve to death. Who does all the cooking? Who does all the cleaning? And all the washing? Who does all the, er, er . . . '

'Bragging?' Enoch offered with a smirk on his face.

Rosie glared at him. 'No. No. Not bragging, er, er, looking after the house,' she said in triumph.

'Who?' Herbert asked as he lost his balance and fell into a pile of steaming rhubarb fodder.

'Us women. That's who,' Rosie said forcefully. Herbert regained his position on the fence and sat surrounded by flies.

'We also tend the sick,' Margaret joined in, 'And have babies.'

'Huh,' Enoch sneered, 'Anyone can have babies. That's not clever.'

'You can't,' Rosie sneered.

'I could if I wanted one.'

'Don't talk daft,' Margaret jeered, 'Only women can have babies. Not men.'

'Oh yes?' Alan said, 'Well, what about gardeners?'

'What about them?' Rosie questioned.

'Who grows the gooseberry bushes? Men. Who makes sure the baby flowers on the bushes are alright? Men. Who pick the babies when they are ripe? Men. See, growing babies is dead easy. It's looking after the gooseberry bushes. That's the hard part. All you women do is tickle the babies' chins and push them about in prams and complain about sleepless nights and teething troubles. You're a right set of moaners.'

Rosie sat staring at Alan. Indignation, frustration, and anger fought to burst out.

'If it wasn't for us men and our tools there wouldn't be any babies at all in this world at large of ours,' Brian added wisely.

'Yer,' Enoch agreed, 'We look after our tools. Our tools are the most important things we've got. Without them there wouldn't be much baby growing or rhubarb growing going off, I can tell you. So don't you women think you're more important than us tool-swinging men.'

'He's got the scarecrow to stand up,' Herbert suddenly said, then added, 'Oh no, he hasn't. It's fallen over again.' The gang looked across to where Mr. Parker was throwing his cap at the prone figure and cursing most horribly.

'That's a good word,' Barry said in appreciation, 'I must remember that one,' and filed it away in his mind under 'curses and swear words for special occasions.'

They watched Mr. Parker struggle to lift the scarecrow into an upright position once again. He turned, bent and stretched to reach an anchoring stone. A sudden breeze caught the vacant-faced figure. It slipped from his hand, wrapped the empty sleeves of its jacket about the old gardener's face, and together they disappeared from view under the large rhubarb leaves, amid fresh Anglo-saxon utterances. A crow in a nearby elm tree fell from its perch in hysterics.

'He's not having much luck is he?' Barry observed.

Brian shook his head then said, 'What he needs is a big cannon. That would scare the birds away and it would be more fun for him. He could pretend he was at war and blast away all day. That would pass his time away in the twilight of his old ageness.'

'Land mines and trip wires would be better,' Enoch joined in. 'Tons better and more spectacle.'

'Four machine-guns. One at each corner of the allotment. That would put the wind up the crows,' Alan offered.

'Hark at this lot,' Rosie said archly, 'Anyone would think World War Three was going on instead of just trying to scare a few scabby crows.'

'Listen,' Enoch said firmly, 'Listen. Protecting crops is very important. I mean, if you wasn't firm with God's wild-life, whoosh, bang. Before you knew what had happened they would take over from us human beans. Then what?'

'Scarehumans,' Alan said blandly.

'What?' Enoch asked.

'Scarehumans. The fields would be full of scarehumans, instead of scarecrows.'

'Eh? Oh yes,' Enoch agreed, 'I see what you mean.' He gave Alan a sideways look, unsure as to whether Alan was serious or just being sarcastic. Alan continued to gaze across the sea of rhubarb with a blank expression on his face. Herbert gave a whimpering cry, resigned himself to his fate, and toppled backwards into the manure once again.

'Do you like doing that?' Barry asked, as he watched Herbert reclimb the fence.

Herbert gave him a disgusted look then said, 'Oh yes, it's wonderful. All my life I've wanted to be a manure diver. I've trained long hours to become perfect at it. You should see me. Show me a pile of manure and I'll be there, diving in. I'd travel the world for a good pile to dive into. Burke.'

'Oh,' Barry answered, 'Still, I suppose it takes all sorts to make up life's pattern that is full of richness.' Herbert tightened his lips and scowled at Barry who sat smirking.

'Come on,' Enoch suddenly said, jumping from the fence, 'Let's go and watch Mr. Chippinghouse drowning worms.'

The gang slipped from their perches and amid much aimless stone throwing and bush lashing with their personal sticks, they made their way to where Mr. Chippinghouse sat by the side of the static water reservoir, staring intently at the end of his fishing rod, and dreaming of catching a fresh trout from the barren, polluted water.

'Hello, Mr. Chippinghouse,' Brian said brightly, as the gang formed a human, semi-circular fence, around the optimistic fisherman.

Mr. Chippinghouse closed his eyes and sighed at the sound of Brian's voice. 'What do you bloody lot want?' he asked.

'We've come to watch your expertness at killing fish,' Rosie said with a hint of reproach in her voice.

'What bait are you using, Mr. Chippinghouse?' Enoch enquired.

'Worms.'

'Have you caught any fish yet?' Alan asked.

'No.'

'Why?' Brian wanted to know.

'Because I keep getting distracted by daft questions,' Mr. Chippinghouse replied.

'Who keeps asking you daft questions, Mr. Chippinghouse?' Barry asked.

'You lot.'

'Ooow. That's a lie.' Margaret protested, 'We've not asked you any daft questions today at all.'

'Look,' the fisherman menaced, 'Clear off. I'm busy.'

'Your float has just moved, Mr. Chippinghouse,' Enoch said excitedly. The fisherman's head jerked back to look at the bright red tip which sat motionless in the still water.

'Oh, it's stopped now,' Enoch added, 'But it moved a few seconds ago. I bet it was a big fish and you missed it, Mr. Chippinghouse.'

Mr. Chippinghouse reeled his line in, stood, lifted his creaking fishing basket, collected his tin of bait, then turning on the gang, hissed, 'I'm moving to the other side of the pond. If you lot follow me I'll skin you all alive.' They watched as he circled the green water, then, placing his basket to the damp ground once more, he cast into the unproductive pool. 'Remember what I said,' he shouted across the water to them.

'Ssshh,' Rosie bawled, 'You'll frighten the fishes.' Mr. Chippinghouse raised his arm and shook his fist at them.

'Uh,' Brian remarked, 'That's not a very friendly gesture to make to us innocent children.'

'No it isn't, Brian,' Rosie agreed.

'Especially since we have made a special journey to keep him company,' Brian went on.

'Quiet right, Brian,' Margaret supported.

'I hope he falls in and drowns or something,' Brian said, 'That would teach him to be kind to children of a nervous dispensation.'

The gang all nodded their heads in agreement, then turning, wandered back to the bombed-site and their favourite den.

Smashing Roman Times

* *

'FRIENDS, Romans and country people. Bend me your ears. I come to bury Julian, not to praise him.' Rosie stood on an up-turned dustbin in the middle of Mrs. Bacon's yard with an off-white, torn bed sheet draped around her shoulders and a leg of her infamous navy blue knickers flapping around her plaster-covered knee cap. Her eyes glittered with passion as she gazed down at the circle of disinterested gang members.

'For Julian was a noble man who never did anybody harm in all 'is entire life. He was a good man who liked fiddling whilst the Fire Brigade put out house fires all over Rome. That is why we, as his citizens, should praise him forever. He also liked wild animals and things, and he was always going to the pictures. You could see him every Saturday, queuing to go into the Coliseum. They showed great films in them days. So, fellow Romans, lend me your ears just like Julian's friend, whose name I've forgotten, did.'

'What's she going on about?' Enoch asked Alan, as he attempted to lower a wingless bluebottle, which was secured by a piece of black cotton, down the smelly, backyard grate.

'I think she wants to borrow a pair of tabs from somebody.'

'What for?' Enoch asked absent mindedly.

'Don't know. But you know Rosie, she's always trying to get things off people.'

'Well, she's not having my earholes,' Enoch replied, 'Besides, she's already got one good pair. Why does she want four ears?'

'Don't know.'

'Huh.' Enoch muttered, then watched as the bluebottle resigned itself to its mission of seeking out secret subterranean tunnels and shafts for its master.

Suddenly Rosie's voice rose by eighty decibels and she bellowed with passion, 'Beware of Ida Marsh.'

'Bloody 'eck,' Enoch jumped and exclaimed. 'Why are you shouting?'

'Beware of Ida Marsh.' Rosie stared with wide eyes and repeated her warning.

'Who's she?' Enoch asked, 'And anyway, who are you supposed to be?'

'I,' Rosie said archly, 'I am Mark Anthony.'

'That's daft,' Enoch shot back. 'You can't be two people. You're either Mark or Tony. You can't be Mark and Tony. That's daft, is that.'

'No,' Rosie replied, with exasperation beginning to tighten her lips. 'No. Not Mark and Tony. Mark Anthony. That's his name. Mark Anthony. He was Julian Caesar's best friend and he stabbed him to deathness.'

'Huh,' Enoch sniffed, 'Not much of a friend if you ask me. Stabbing his best friend Julian.'

'They were always at it in them days,' Brian piped up. 'Stabbing and nailing persons who believed in God to pieces of wood. And they chucked Christians in white frocks to lions. And they made slaves row boats at full speed for years on end while a man practiced on his drum. And they were always holding races in their charities.'

'Oh,' Enoch exclaimed, then turning to check on the progress of his fearless Bluebottle, said, 'They kept themselves busy, didn't they?'

'Yes, they did.' Rosie replied firmly, 'That's why they conquered this world at large of ours.'

'Who did?' Herbert asked as he climbed over the wall which divided the terraced houses and joined the gang, 'And why are you standing on the bin?'

'The Romans,' Rosie turned and answered, 'And this isn't a bin, it's my podium and I'm Mark Anthony.'

'Who's he?' Herbert wanted to know.

Alan lifted his head from watching the bluebottle, which was testing the temperature of the sewer water, and said, 'She sez he was Julian Caesar's best friend and he killed him with a dagger.'

'Huh. Some friend.' Herbert sniffed.

'That's just what I said.' Enoch agreed.

'Did he always stand on a poe?' Herbert asked Rosie.

Rosie's face tightened. She put her hands on her hips and then glared at the chuckling trio. 'Burkes,' she hissed, then turning to the other gang members, addressed them. 'Take no notice of them three. All they are good at is drowning flies. Now, where was I?' Rosie took up the stance of Mark Anthony once more and continued her oration.

'Yes, good citizens of Roman town. Beware of Ida Marsh.' Then added in a confidential tone, 'She was Julian's wife, you know.'

'Well why didn't they call her Ida Caesar, then?' Enoch called.

'Because,' Rosie said through clenched teeth, 'Because. Er. Because. Julian didn't want anybody to know he was married. I mean. You know how women go off married heroes once they find out they are married. Don't they?'

Margaret, who had a great aversion to married heroes, nodded her head vigorously in support of Rosie's explanation. Rosie beamed a smile as a thank-you, then continued. 'Oh, yes. Beware of Ida Marsh alright. She's a right troublecauser. Do you know, she's caused more rows between Julian and the other Romans than anyone else. So watch out for her and her tongue that is always lashing about.'

'He's dead.' Alan said.

'No he's not.' Enoch replied.

'Yes he is.' Rosie shouted.

'How do you know?' Enoch asked.

'Because he's been dead for hundreds of years.'

'Well he was twitching his little legs two minutes ago.' Enoch shouted back.

'Oh,' Rosie said and blushed in confusion, 'I thought you meant Julian Caesar. Not your fly.'

Enoch shook his head in pitying disgust. 'I sometimes wonder if she's right in the head,' he murmured to Alan and Herbert. They nodded in agreement.

'We'd best find another one.' Enoch announced, and the three crossed to the outside lavatory to hunt inside for bluebottles or daddy long-legs.

Rosie was grateful to see them go and sighing with satisfaction she returned to her collection of scruffy senators. 'It is now time, good citizens of Roman town, to pass some laws. Law One. No citizen must in future torment the lions in their cages. This will let them get on with their job of eating Christians.

'Law two. Anybody not rowing fast enough on the galleons will be smacked very hard. And Law Three. Now that Julian is dead I should become your new leader.'

There was a muffled yell and a smashing sound from the far lavatory as Enoch, who had been balancing precariously on the seatless rim of the lavatory bowl, slipped and shattered it into a thousand pieces. For some seconds all was deathly quiet, then suddenly Alan's voice quavered in a ghostly manner from within the lavatory, 'Beware of Ida Marsh.'

'Never mind bloody Ida Marsh.' Enoch's voice sounded, 'Beware of old lass Bacon. Come on. We'd best be off.' The three fly-catchers emerged from the devastated lavatory covered in a mixture of white distemper and lavatory-pan water. With a furtive glance towards Mrs. Bacon's kitchen window, they fled past the group of open-mouthed senators and disappeared up the entry towards the sanctuary of the street.

*   *   *   *

Some time later, as the gang sat on the creosoted bunk beds in Barry's air-raid shelter, having deemed it the safest place to be should Rosie's dad decide to blitz them when he discovered the stump of the lavatory bowl poking from the ground, Brian remarked, 'This must be how the Christians felt when the Romans were hunting them.'

'Yer,' Enoch said with feeling, 'Mind you, I bet the Christians didn't go around breaking Roman lavatories, though."

'No.' Alan sighed and glanced out of the door at the beckoning sunshine. 'Prisoners. That's what we are. Prisoners in our own country. And all because of a piddling lavatory. Huh. It's not fair. I mean anyone could break a lavatory. After all they are only made of pot. Why can't they make them of steel or concrete? That would be much better. And safer.'

'I don't see what you lot are moaning about,' Rosie said indignantly, 'It's our house that is lavatory-less. Not yours. I mean, what are we going to use until Dad gets a new one?'

No-one answered. 'Typical,' Rosie said in disgust.

'Look,' Margaret suddenly said, 'I'm fed up with all this talk of lavs. Let's talk about something else to pass the time of our lives away.'

Each one suggested various topics but their minds were too preoccupied with thoughts of vengeance-seeking Mr. Bacon to concentrate for long. And so they lapsed into silence and sat swinging their legs on the edge of the bare bunks.

'I bet this is how the Christians felt just before lion-chucking time,' Enoch sighed.

'I wonder if they drew lots to see who went first?' Alan asked.

'Suppose so. I mean, the first one to be chucked would stand no chance. But as the lions got full, well, the last over the side might stand a chance of escaping. Wouldn't he?'

'Yes.' the gang agreed.

'It would be the same when it came to nailing them to lumps of wood. Wouldn't it? I mean. Perhaps they would run out of nails,' Brian offered.

'Or wood.' Herbert added. The gang nodded wisely.

'It must have been dead rough being a Christian in them days.' Margaret said. 'What do you mean. In them days.' Herbert spoke, 'It's not much fun in these days. Not with roamin' Mr. Bacon on the prowl looking for us.'

Rosie agreed. Even though she was his off-spring she knew her father maintained complete impartiality when it came to dealing out oaths, death threats, and punishment. He treated the gang as a complete entity, not as individuals. And so she sat tight along with her fellow conspirators in the comparative safety of Barry's overgrown air-raid shelter, whilst her father patrolled the streets carrying invisible lumps of wood. A hammer. Bags of nails. And with a hundred lions straining at the leash. In short, Rosie knew there was safety in numbers and which side her bread was margarined.

'What's the time?' Enoch asked generally.

Barry poked his head out of the doorway, glanced up at the sun, noted the angle in relation to the roof-tops, and said, 'Seven-and-a-half minutes past four.'

'Flippin' 'eck,' Margaret exclaimed, 'We've been sat in here ages. The coast must be clear by now. Why don't we risk it and go to our den? At least the air will be fresher.'

They all looked at each other and a silent agreement was reached. One by one the gang stealthily slipped into the open, ran across the yard and bursting out onto the deserted street they flew across the ruins until they reached the safety of the hollow which was their den.

'We'd better post a look-out,' Alan said breathlessly, and as on all such occasions, Margaret was forcibly chosen. The gang sat on their individual house-bricks, and passing a stick of liquorice root around, they all took their regulation four sucks.

'It's better out here, isn't it?' Herbert remarked, 'It's better to be under God's sky than in a smelly air-raid shelter waiting to be chucked to lions.'

'Yer.' the gang all agreed.

'I bet them there Christians would have been glad of that shelter though. Smell and all,' Enoch said.

'Well, yes. I suppose so.' Herbert conceded.

'Oh yes,' Enoch continued, 'I bet if there had been air-raid shelter builders around in them far-off days of Roman times, he'd have made stacks of money flogging them to the Christians. And I bet he'd have made steel lavatories to match as well. Not like us. We have to put up with daft pot ones and all the haphazardness that goes with them.'

'Yes. Like wobbly seats and smashability,' Brian supported. 'It's not fair.' The gang shook their heads in agreement at this wise statement.

All, that is, except Rosie, who suddenly exclaimed, 'I've just remembered. We're having fish and chips for tea.'

'So?' Enoch said in puzzlement.

'Well I'm supposed to fetch them,' Rosie replied.

'Rather you than me,' Enoch said with feeling.

'What do you mean? It's your fault we're in this trouble in the first place. You and your daft fly catching. If it wasn't for you we would all be free and not in hiding from my dad.' Rosie exploded.

'Wow. That's it. I've just had an idea to get us out of this mess.' Enoch exclaimed.

'What is it?' Barry questioned.

'Rosie is our way out.'

'How?' Herbert asked.

'Well, Rosie has got to fetch the chips, right?'

'Yer.'

'Well all she has got to do is to tell her dad that on her way back she saw this burglar climbing out of their front room window and she chased him to save the famberly jewels, and that she chased him into their lavatory and in the noble struggle to capture him he kicked the lavatory over and escaped from her. That way Rosie will be a hero to her dad and we will be free. It's brilliant.'

'He'll never believe that.' Rosie scorned.

'Of course he will. You're a smashing story-teller Rosie. He's bound to believe you.'

Using vast amounts of cajoling Rosie became convinced of her unique ability, and so with a much relieved heart she set off to the fish and chip shop,leaving an elated gang in the den.

*　　*　　*　　*

All the way home Rosie rehearsed her unlikely story, refining it, adding four more villains, dropping them in favour of a german spy, executing him and promoting a mass killer, until finally she reached the top of the entry which led to her backyard. She took a deep breath, then, with pounding heart she approached the kitchen door. She paused for a moment to let her mind flash through the salient details of the story, took another deep breath, and reached for the door handle. The door shot open even before her hand closed on the knob and there, standing before her, was the towering bulk of her glaring father.

'Who's smashed our bloody lavatory,' he bellowed.

Rosie stood trembling. The mass killer escaped. The story crumbled. Here before her was threatening reality.

'It wasn't me, Dad. Honest,' she blurted out. 'Honest it wasn't me. It was Enoch Thompson. Honest.'

Her father clenched his teeth and fists. He took a determined breath. His eyes narrowed and has he shot from the doorway, loosening his thick leather belt, he roared, 'I'll give him Enoch Thompson when I catch him. I'll crucify the little sod.'

Rosie watched her rampaging father disappear up the entry and sighed a great sigh of relief. Then, with her father's threatening words echoing in her head, she turned to enter the house and suddenly thought, 'Crucify him? Perhaps there is some Roman blood in our famberly after all.'

School of Scoundrels

* *

'I SAY YOU CHAPS, what ho, toodle pip,' Alan said, 'Welcome to Tom Brown's School Days, school.' Enoch and Barry looked at him quizzically and grunted.

'Where's the tucking in shop?' Enoch asked.

'Oh, that. What ho. It's over by the school dorms,' Alan informed them cheerily.

'What's them?' Barry asked.

'It's where we kip,' Alan answered, 'You know, where the beds are.'

'Oh,' Barry said.

'Oh yes, you'll like it here at Tommy Brown's School. We're all upper-crust and dead rich, you know. We're from the hoy-po-loy class.'

'Can you lend us some money then?' Enoch, the opportunist, asked eagerly.

'Fraid not, old bean,' Alan answered, 'I'm skint, don't you know.'

'I thought you said you were dead rich.'

'Well, yes, I am. But it's a rule of us upper-crust-richies, that we don't lend money to them that needs it,' Alan replied.

'Can't see much point in lending money to them that don't need it,' Barry sniffed.

'I don't mek the rich rules,' Alan flared. 'Besides, if you've just come to our rich school, you must have money of your own. And also, we consider it a bad form to talk about our money, don't you know.'

'Oh,' Barry said.

'So, if you'll pick up your hampers and suitcases, I'll tek you to your dorms,' Alan smiled.

Enoch and Barry lifted their invisible luggage and followed Alan a short distance to a hollow on the bombed-site.

'Here we are, toodle pip. This is your hole of resi-dance. Comfy, isn't it? What ho. Old beans.'

'Yer,' Enoch said looking around, 'I can't wait to start toasting our crumpets for tea.'

Alan's smile widened. 'Oh yes, you'll get plenty of crumpet here at Tommy Brown's School Day's school. We're at it every night. We practically live on school crumpet. If you run out of them, you can buy some more at the tucking in shop which is run by Mrs. Pikelet.'

Barry giggled.

'You mustn't laugh at her name. Rosie, I mean, Mrs. Pikelet, gets ever so upset if you laugh.' Alan informed them. 'Well, I'll leave you now to get settled in. I'm off to play rugby against a wall. It's a great life here at Tommy Brown's school. Toodle pip.'

'Toodle pip.' Enoch replied.

'See,' Alan said, 'You're getting used to our rich ways already. You've started toodle pipping, and you haven't been here five minutes.'

Barry wasn't going to be left out and so he gave Alan a toodle pip and a what ho, and a don't you know. Then for good measure threw in a jolly old bean. Alan was suitably impressed.

Enoch thought 'How easily the working classes are seduced by thoughts of money' or put ting it another way, 'Barry's crawling to the rich again.'

Alan turned and retraced his steps to his imaginary encounter on the playing fields of eaten.

'It's nice at this school,' Barry said, as they sat eating crumpets that looked suspiciously like bread and jam.

'It's alright,' Enoch sniffed. 'Mind you, if it's not nice at a dead rich school, where is it nice, I'd like to know?'

'It was good of them to let us in though, wasn't it?' Barry said. 'After all, we do come from the background of the worker's class.'

'They only let us in because we're dead brainy,' Enoch replied.

'They need our brains, that's all. Don't let 'em kid you. Once they've used our brain boxes, they'll not talk to us any more. You watch. My Dad sez the dead rich wear out the soul cases of the working man, then chuck them on the scrap heap of life's experience. We're but tools of capitalist ray-jeans.'

'Oh,' Alan said in puzzlement. 'Still, we have got the high jinks and the boating on the river, and banging our tankards on the school dinner table, to look forward to.'

'Suppose so,' Enoch said despondently. He had already worked himself into a state of homesickness, despite the fact that he was less than two hundred yards from his terraced house. Suddenly Rosie's voice bawled across the ruins. 'If any school boys from Tom Brown's School Days school want any more crumpet they'd better hurry up. I'm closing me crumpet shop in a minute. Don't you know.'

'Do you fancy some more crumpets.' Barry asked.

Ever-hungry Enoch nodded his head vigorously, and, cramming the last of the bread and jam into his mouth, stood and followed Barry towards Mrs. Pikelet's tuck shop hole.

'Well, pon my soul, bless me, and what a to-do,' Rosie exclaimed as they entered her shop. 'What have we here? Two boys who are new to Tom Brown's School, I'll be bound up. And what can I do for you smart gents?'

'We want some crumpet, Mrs. Pikelet,' Barry said.

Enoch giggled. Rosie flashed a menacing look in his direction, recovered herself, and beaming at Barry, said, 'Well, young school-gent. I've only got four left. Is that enough to feed your healthy rich apple-tight?'

'We're not rich,' Enoch stated. 'We're poor working class persons who have got into this rich school by the sweat of our brow and the honest toil of our hands that are worn out wiv work.'

'Oh,' Rosie exclaimed, 'Well, if you're poor, you can't have any crumpet.'

'Typical.' Enoch sniffed.

'I've got some money, Mrs. Pikelet,' Barry said 'I'll pay for all four of your delicious crumpets. I will give two to my school chump, and eat two myself.'

'I don't want charity from a rich school kid.' Enoch flared. 'If I want crumpet, I'll buy it with money I've earned by the sweat of my brow.'

'It's only pretend,' Barry whispered, 'There's no need to get upset.'

Enoch re-entered the reality of fantasy. 'Oh, er, oh, yes, Mrs. Pikelet,' Enoch said, 'I will take the last of your crumpet off your hands for you. Here is my money.' Enoch held out the invisible coins.

'You can't have them,' Rosie said archly, 'I've just sold them to this nice rich school boy who has good manners.' Enoch's eyes narrowed. His mouth tightened, and hate shone from his eyes.

Rosie stood smirking at him. 'There we are, young sir,' she said, turning to Barry, 'Four of my very best crumpets.'

'Thanks, Mrs. Pikelet,' Barry answered, taking the imaginary food from Rosie's hands.

'Ah, well. It's shutting-up-shop time,' Rosie sighed, 'It's the end of another busy crumpet-cooking day here at Tommy Brown's School. Off you go, young gents. You'd better be in bed before the school bell tolls the parting of Nelly, otherwise the big boys will burn your bum in front of the fire.'

'I'd like to see them try,' Enoch snapped.

Ten minutes later it was morning. All the gang, with the exception of Margaret and Rosie, sat around a plank of wood, which was supported by house-bricks at each corner. They were banging the board with empty tin cans and 'What Ho-ing' all over the place.

'Ha. Ha. Ha.' Brian laughed falsely, 'I see Smith the Miner is up to his usual planks. What Oh!'

'Yes,' Alan agreed, 'He is a card, isn't he? Always full of jelly grapes and mischief. I bet he grows up from this public school to become the prime minister or something else.'

'Yes,' Brian replied, 'He's very popular with the big boys. They like him because he's always giving them a fag. They only have to shout "Fag", and good old Smith the Miner is there, handing 'em round.'

'What I want to know is, what's a Miner named Smith doing at a money bags school. And why is he wasting his cigarette ration on a bunch of toffee noses.' Enoch asked. 'He should be down a pit, digging coal for England, not living it up at a rich kids school. And another thing. He's got as much chance of becoming the prime minister as, as a snowball in hell has of passing through the eye of a Camel's needle.'

'Randy MacDonald was a prime minister and he was once a miner,' Alan said.

'It wasn't Randy MacDonald,' Brian sneered, 'You're getting mixed up. It was old MacDonald. You know. Him who had a farm and He-Hi'd all over the place. They made him prime minister because he came from the land of gentry. I don't know, Alan, you always get hold of the wrong end of the stick.'

Alan didn't argue but turned to re-join the others to continue banging his tankard on the ancient school table.

Rosie crossed into the hollow. She was wearing a shoe box on her head and around her shoulders was a piece of torn black-out curtain. 'Boys. Boys.' she shouted, 'Settle down.'

The tankard banging ceased. Rosie gazed around the table. 'Ha, ah. I see we have two new richies who have come to our world-famous learning school. I hope you've brought your money with you.'

'What's Mrs. Pikelet doing dressed as the headmaster?' Enoch asked Barry.

'She wanted to play the part. She fought Alan for it, and won.'

'Oh,' Enoch said, then as an afterthought added, 'Well I'm not teking orders from her. If she starts bossing me about there's going to be a new headmaster at this school, pretty quick.'

Rosie heard Enoch's comment and quickly made a mental note to steer clear of the new boy. She wanted to hang on to her power for as long as possible. To further ensure this she announced grandly, 'It is a tradition of Tommy Brown's School Day's school that all new boys can have free crumpet for a whole month and also they can please themselves what they do until they settle in.' From the corner of her eye she saw Enoch beam with satisfaction. Rosie sighed inwardly and realised her job was safe for the time being at least.

'Right boys,' she continued, 'I have some notices to read out to you.' She rustled some pieces of old newspaper, glanced around, and began to 'read.'

'I first have some very sad news to tell you. One of our old boys who was at this school before any of you lot was twinkling in your mothers' eyes, has got himself shot. He was a great sportsman at this school and won us ever so many cups and prizes. He was also a smashing big boy and wasn't stingey with his money. I think we should all take a lesson from him and give this great school of ours as much money as you can.' She looked up but saw only blank faces. A twinge of disappointment shot through her as she realised that her first attempt at prising the pupil's pocket money away from them had failed. She began attempt number two.

'The school is holding a collection of your money to have a lump of stone carved with his name on it. This will help us all to remember him in the future. I hope you will all give the school a bit of your money for this.' She paused and gazed at them again. Still blank faces. Rosie's second attempt had failed. She launched into her final plan.

'The school is going to hold a raffle to get money for the big boy who had laid his life down fighting Germans on foreign soil that is for ever England. I hope you'll all buy a ticket from me. Please.'

The gang shuffled uneasily on their house-bricks. Rosie had hit a weak spot, albeit below the belt. It smacked of patriotic blackmail.

'What did they call the big boy?' Alan asked grudgingly.

'Jones the Miner,' Rosie answered eagerly.

'Not another bloody miner,' Enoch exclaimed, 'This school is full of pit workers. If I'd have known it was full of workers' classes I wouldn't have joined. I'm not paying good money out for a lump of stone with a miner's name on it. That's the trouble with the workers' classes, they think us richies are made of money that grows on trees.'

The gang muttered in agreement.

Rosie glared at Enoch, her mind racing to find a solution that would keep their thoughts on giving and not keeping. 'Boys, boys,' she shouted, 'Remember our poor soldiers who are fighting up their fronts and are losing legs and arms left, right and centre. Think of them as well as Jones the Miner.'

Rosie was punching unfairly now. Fouling at every turn.

Enoch parried the verbal blows. 'All that lot didn't come to this school. We can't pay everybody you know. It's enough forking out for Jones the Miner.'

'Alright,' Rosie said quickly, 'We'll settle for him. Now give us your money.'

Before they knew what was happening they were all digging in their grubby pockets and handing over half pennies and pennies to the open-handed headmaster. Rosie quickly gathered the donations and then said hurriedly,

'Thank you boys. I must go to my studying room now. Margaret is your teacher for today. She will now learn you things.'

Margaret crossed to the gang and began to address them, whilst Rosie, with a furtive glance over her shoulder, made her way to the crumpet shop hole.

Enoch sat thoughtfully. Rosie had pulled a fast one but his mind hadn't caught up with the intricacy of the scheme. He glanced towards the crumpet shop and was just in time to see Rosie disappearing towards the street. He decided to follow her. With a casual, 'Well I'm going to the rugby field,' he stood and quickly crossed the bombed-site towards the distant figure. Rosie stopped, looked round guiltily, then entered Mr. Chippinghouse's corner shop. Enoch slipped into a nearby entry and waited.

Rosie left the shop some five minutes later clutching a white paper bag. Enoch watched her approaching his hiding place and as she drew level he stepped out. 'Hello, Rosie.'

Rosie jumped and then stood, flustered. 'Er. Hello, Enoch,' she answered nervously.

'What you got in the bag?' he asked.

'Nothing,' she replied, holding the bag close to her chest.

'You've used the raffle money to buy spice. Haven't you?'

Rosie protested her innocence for quite a while, then, when she saw Enoch didn't believe her, blurted out, 'If you don't tell anybody, Enoch, I'll share the sweets with you.'

Enoch smirked and said, 'OK, Rosie.'

Together they crossed the road and going down a path towards the allotments, eventually reached a dilapidated garden hut. After carefully looking around, they slipped quietly inside to share the ill-gotten gains.

Enoch's school career progressed at a swift pace. He became head boy and, by mid-afternoon, had ousted Margaret to become the chief teacher. Rosie reluctantly assisted in his promotion until tea-time arrived. She was then publicly denounced and left the school in disgrace.

'Right,' Enoch the headmaster said, 'The rest of the day is a holiday. Let's go and play war on the bombed-site.'

The gang all cheered and threw their tankards in the air. Tommy Brown's School Days school fell into disrepair.

No Escape

* *

'**L**ADIES and genklemen, Whodinti will now escape from his world-famous potato sack which will contain himself and the ferocious wild dog, Blackie. Please watch carefully, ladies and genklemen, as Whodinti battles inside the sack with Blackie, whilst doing his escaping act. Fank you.'

Rosie stood holding the dirty sack open as Enoch thrust Blackie, Mrs. Johnson's friendly and good natured mongrel, into it. Enoch turned and faced the motley audience of disinterested neighbourhood kids.

'Ladies and genklemen,' he addressed them, 'I am now about to climb into my fainemous sack from which there is no escape, but from which I will. Please note that during my escape I will be pestered and probably mauled savagely by this wild, untamed animal, Blackie.'

Blackie's head poked from the neck of the sack and panted and beamed in excitement at this new game that the funny little two-legged pink things had thought up for him. His tail wagged in high excitement.

'Do you have the bandages and blood-stopping ointment handy, my assistant?' Enoch asked grandly.

Rosie made a great show of holding up some dirty strips of linen and a jar of Vaseline.

'Fank you,' Enoch said, 'I will now climb into my world-fainemous escaping sack.'

Rosie held the neck lower and Enoch placed one foot inside, Blackie bounded around the restricting interior, delirious with happiness and excitement. With an awkward, unbalanced hop, Enoch's other foot was over the edge and he stood unsteadily with his arms above his head.

'Have you the special unbreakable rope, my assistant?' he asked. Rosie reached to the ground and showed the small audience a piece of old, frayed, washing line.

'Ladies and genklemen, I will now disappear from the view and my assistant will tie up the . . .'

Enoch didn't finish his speech, but lost his footing as Blackie tried to get on more intimate terms with the great escapologist. 'You may tie up the sack,' his muffled, fur-filled voice sounded.

Rosie bunched the neck together and wrapped the line tightly around it, finishing with six granny knots. 'Ladies and genklemen, the sack is now fastened for ever,' she announced grandly.

'Gerroff, Blackie. Stop it,' Enoch's voice said hoarsely.

'Can you hear me, oh mighty Whodinti?' Rosie called.

'Pack it in, Blackie. Ow. Ow,' Enoch gasped.

Rosie kicked the sack. There was a muffled yell. 'I said, can you hear me, Whodinti?' she repeated sternly.

'Yer,' Enoch panted, 'Blackie, get off me shirt tail.'

'One, two, three, go,' Rosie shouted.

The sack became a seething mass of animation as Enoch struggled to find the knife that Rosie had said was in the sack. Blackie was in ecstasy, his wet nose buried in Enoch's trouser pocket. The audience watched as the bundle rolled around the bombed-site hollow, with gasps, yelps, and panting coming from within.

'Flippin' 'eck, me braces are caught on Blackie's collar,' Enoch's muffled voice exclaimed. 'Now pack it in, Blackie.'

One side of the sack bucked in and out in a steady rhythm.

'Get off me back Blackie. Stop it you dirty bugger or I'll murder you. Where's that bloody knife?'

Rosie heard the word knife and colour drained from her face. She glanced to where she had secretly placed it ready to slip into the sack. It still lay behind the house-brick. She knelt quickly to the sack and whispered, 'Enoch. Enoch. Are you there?'

'Of course I am, you silly bugger. Where's the knife? I can't find the bloody knife.'

'It's out here, Enoch,' Rosie whispered.

There was a pause and then an explosion. 'What? What? What did you say?'

'It's out here. I forgot to put it in the sack,' Rosie said. 'Sorry.'

'Sorry?' Enoch screamed. 'Sorry? This flippin' dog is going berserk in here, you know. It's just tiddled down me wellington. And it's licking me to death. Now get me out.'

Rosie stood and faced the now laughing audience. 'Ladies and genklemen,' she announced, 'For once in his life Whodinti cannot get out of his world-famous sack due to his circustanders that he did not know were unforeseen by him. Using my knowledge of rope I will untie his sack for you and then I will . . . '

'Get this bloody sack open, quick,' Enoch interupted with menace. 'Stop nattering. I'm dying alive in here.'

Rosie made a grab and caught the secured neck. It slipped from her grasp as Blackie pawed frenziedly at the side. Once more she caught it and began working on the six knots. The violent struggling had tightened them and she was finding it impossible to free even one.

'Use the flipping knife,' Enoch gasped, 'Hurry up.'

Rosie retrieved it and plunged it into the sacking, drawing it down until a hole appeared. From within Blackie's head arose. He sniffed, barked, and then withdrew to the comforting dark for more romping with his new-found friend.

Enoch groaned as he was smothered in licks once again. His strength was ebbing. With a final effort his hands found the opening and he tore wildly at the hole. He forced his shoulder through and, with a heave, pushed himself free of his world-famous sack, collapsing in the dust and muttering, 'You burke. You big burke.'

Blackie appeared and jumped on Enoch's back. 'Oh no,' Enoch groaned, and then resigned himself to another bout of sniffing, licking and pawing.

The sparse audience stood looking down at Enoch's heaving body. Rosie took charge of the situation and said brightly, 'Ladies and genklemen, I will now bandage the body of the world-famous Whodinti and administer his world-famous blood-stopping ointment.'

Enoch turned his head in the dust, glared at Rosie, and hissed, 'You come near me and I'll murder you.'

Rosie took the hint and kept her distance whilst Enoch continued to recover. Suddenly his eyes were caught by a thin-faced infant who was sidling away from the rest. In his hand he held an empty pop bottle. 'Just a minute,' Enoch shouted, 'You haven't paid.'

The infant turned, sniffed, and called, 'I'm not paying a whole pop bottle to watch that rubbish.'

Enoch sighed and after a while stood and began brushing dust and dog hairs from his tattered clothes. Blackie sat to one side, his keen eyes never leaving his adopted master, anxious for any sign, no matter how small, that he was required for further play.

Brian crossed the bombed-site and looked down on the dishevelled Enoch. 'Have you started?' he asked.

'Have we started?' Enoch exclaimed. 'I've just nearly been finished.'

He glared at Blackie. Blackie barked happily. He glared at Rosie. Rosie smiled sweetly and said, 'Oh Brian, Enoch was ever so brave. You should have seen him. He was a hero. He fought Blackie in the sack, and he won. Didn't you, Enoch?'

'Well, er, er, I suppose so,' Enoch answered.

'And he was smashing at escaping Brian. He's a real hero. He's the best in the gang. Aren't you, Enoch?'

Enoch stood, feeling pride chasing away anger.

'Oh yes, Brian, I bet he can escape from anything in this world of ours. I don't know anyone as good as good old Enoch.' Enoch's pride was now firmly in control as he realised how true Rosie's words were.

'I bet his next escape from the chains and mancanals, what he is going to do now, will be even better. Won't it Enoch?' Rosie asked in a servile voice.

'Oh yes,' Enoch said firmly, 'There's nothing to it.'

'Good,' Rosie said quickly, and turning to the audience announced, 'Ladies and genklemen. Whodinti will now escape from his famous chains and mancanals which are burglar and escape proof. This is a very dangerous trick and Whodinti has asked me to ask you to pay another pop bottle or jam jar if you want to stay and see him dice his deathness.'

Mutterings of dissent came from the audience. One or two turned to follow the thin infant. Rosie saw the danger signs. She glanced at Brian. Brian quickly removed the cardboard plaque which hung down his back, and which he'd tramped the streets with to advertise the great Whodinti. He took a step towards the audience and began his silent, menacing look technique. Soon four more pop bottles were added to the collection of jam jars in the hollow, and the audience stood awaiting the next hair-raising escape.

'Have you got my chains and mancanals?' Whodinti called loudly. Rosie pranced forward holding three lavatory chains and a pair of toy cowboy handcuffs above her head.

'Whodinti is now going to be fastened up in these,' she said to the reluctant audience, 'But first I will blindfold him so that he can't see me doing the dirty deed.'

Using one of the linen strips she bound Enoch's eyes.

'Can you see anything, Whodinti?' she called.

'No. I cannot see a thing, my assistant,' Enoch replied.

'To prove he can't see anything, ladies and genklemen, I will hold up my fingers in front of his face. How many fingers am I holding up Whodinti?'

'I don't know, my assistant. I cannot see 'em.'

Rosie looked at the audience in triumph. The audience looked back at Rosie, variously picking their noses or scratching sundry parts of their bodies.

'And now for the chains,' Rosie shouted.

She quickly secured Enoch's wrists and ankles, finally snapping on the handcuffs.

'To make the trick impossible, ladies and genklemen, I will now secure the end of his ankle chain to this ferocious, wild, untamed animal, Blackie.' She slipped the chain into the dog's collar and then tied it, receiving a thank-you lick on the hand in return. Blackie was once more reunited with his very best friend. Blackie

54

was happy.

'Are you ready, Whodinti?' Rosie called.

'I am ready, my assistant.'

'Ready. Steady. Go.'

Enoch began struggling and twisting his wrists, giving exaggerated pants and groans as he did so. The audience watched intently. Blackie sat with his head cocked to one side, panting in anticipation, awaiting developments.

*　　*　　*　　*

It was a warm evening and Mrs. Brigham's tom cat had begun his ritual, sniffing prowl out on the street which boarded the bombed-site. The majority of smells he knew by heart, but he lived ever-hopeful of discovering a new one. Especially of the female gender. That evening the gods smiled on him. His nose struck oil at the gas lamp. He sniffed, sniffed and sniffed again. He couldn't believe his luck. He purred luxuriously. A shudder of ecstasy rippled through him as he followed his nose along the invisible path of eroticism. All his senses were concentrated on that one goal. The end of the trail. Nothing would bar his way. No obstacle would prevent the fulfilment of his urgent desire. Up tumbled mounds of broken bricks, down dusty bomb-blasted holes, ever onward. Nearer and nearer to his heart's desire.

'Are you free yet, Whodinti?' Rosie enquired theatrically, 'Have the chains released you from your prisoner?'

Enoch was panting and sweating and fast losing his temper.

'Shut your gob, Rosie,' he hissed.

'Ladies and genklemen, Whodinti will be free as a bird at any moment now,' she continued.

The audience was becoming increasingly restless, despite Brian's threatening looks. Rosie realised it would take only one audible complaint and the rest would follow. She was in danger of losing the pop bottles and jam jars.

'Whodinti will now hurry up even faster,' she shouted, 'His festers will be free at any second.'

Enoch's eyes were filling with tears of frustration as the chains continued to hold him in bondage.

A tiny, creeping, ginger ball of fur entered the corner of Blackie's eyes. Instinctively his neck stiffened. Slowly his head lowered, his eyes fastened onto the target, and a growl gathered strength in his throat.

The cat sniffed onwards and nearer.

Blackie's legs coiled, his muscles tightened, then with lightning speed he unwound and threw himself up and out of the hollow. Enoch's feet shot from under him. For a fraction of a second he hung parallel to the ground, then with a bewildered look on his face, he crashed down in the dust. The force of the sudden pull snapped his ankle chains.

'Ladies and genklemen,' Rosie shouted excitedly, 'The great Whodinti's feet are free. Look. What did I tell you? I said he was fantastic.'

Enoch lay blindfolded and manacled on the ground, cursing Blackie who was now a tiny dot as he pursued the cat across the ruins.

'What about his hands?' a voice squeaked.

Brian spun to confront the objector but already other voices were shouting dissent. Rosie began to panic quietly to herself. 'Ladies and genklemen, if you want to see him undo his hands it's another jam jar each.'

There were cried of 'Rubbish, bugger off,' and other polite suggestions until eventually the audience dispersed across the ruins, leaving Brian, Rosie, and restrained Enoch alone in the hollow.

Rosie crossed to Enoch and roughly pulled down his blindfold. 'They've all gone,' she said sullenly.

Enoch sniffed and looked down at his scratched legs and grazed knees. Brian began freeing his hands until the chains were uncoiled. Enoch rubbed his sore wrists. 'How much have we made?' he asked as he continued sitting in the centre of the hollow. Rosie crossed to the hole she had made from loose house-bricks, and began counting the jam jars and pop bottles. 'One-and-fourpence ha'penny,' she said, 'That's fivepence ha'penny each.'

Enoch brightened.

Suddenly from the top of the hollow there came a loud single bark.

They looked up. Blackie stood on the lip of the hole, his tail wagging furiously, a wide grin splitting his face at finding his little pink friend again.

'Oh, no,' Enoch groaned.

With a bound that brought down half the side of the hollow, and another which caved in Rosie's hole and smashed the jam jars and pop bottles, Blackie threw himself on Enoch and licked and nuzzled him in ecstasy.

Enoch lay, too weak to resist, the sound of his profits being destroyed ringing in his ears, realising that this was one ordeal from which Whodinti could never escape.

A Rare World Record

'WE'RE growing beans on pink blotting paper', Rosie informed the gang one afternoon as they watched Alan balancing on one leg on an upturned bucket.

'What for?' Enoch asked, his eyes never leaving Alan.

'To watch the miracle of Mother Nature making a seed grow', Rosie answered.

'Why?' Brian enquired, as he silently strained his brain, willing Alan to lose his balance,

'To understand where beans come from', Rosie informed him.

'We know where they come from', Herbert replied, 'They come out of a tin from the corner shop.'

'No, not tinned beans, before that. When they are growing in the fields and are at one with the bosom of Mother Nature.'

'That's a swear word,' Enoch remarked absent-mindedly.

'What is?' Rosie asked

'Bosom. It's a swear word.'

'No, it's not', Rosie flared, 'It's a science word for the ground, is bosom.'

'Well, it sounds a bit earthy to me.' Barry chuckled.

Rosie made a face at Barry's back and then got on with her task of tormenting a blue-bottle which she had adopted and housed in a jam jar. She bent her face close to the glass and said quietly, 'One day, Mr. Blue-bottle, you will go to sleep in crystal liz and wake up with beautiful red and gold wings. Then you will be a lovely butterfly.'

'That's caterpillars.' Margaret said.

'What is?' Rosie queried.

'Caterpillars turn into butterflies. Blue-bottles don't,' Margaret answered. 'Blue-bottles turn into . . . er . . . er.'

'Dead blue-bottles,' Enoch said. Rosie glared at Enoch's bent back.

'How many have I done?' Alan asked as he wobbled on the bucket.

'Eighty-four.' Herbert answered.

'I've done more than that.' Alan protested. 'What's the record?'

'One hundred and fifty-three', Herbert replied.

Alan wobbled afresh, screwed his face in forced concentration, and continued his assault on the world record for one-legged bucket standing. Herbert silently lost count for the fourth time, and started again.

'I think I'll call my pet blue-bottle er . . . er . . . Buzzy.' Rosie announced. 'Do you like your new name, Buzzy?' She tapped the side of the jam jar. The fly buzzed obligingly. 'He does,' Rosie beamed. 'Ah, isn't he sweet?'

'Tommy Conway ties bits of cotton to blue-bottles and pins the other end to his pullover,' Barry said with a smirk. 'He's daft, as well.'

Rosie's mouth tightened, she narrowed her eyes, and tried to burn a hole in Barry's back with them. 'I wish I was a witch', she thought.

'We're growing mustard and cress on a flannel.' Margaret informed the gang of adjudicators.

'We did that last year in nature study,' Enoch answered, 'And we bisected a sheep's eye.'

'Ugh', Rosie exclaimed, 'That's disgusting.'

'No, it's not.' Enoch replied. 'You have to find out how things work in this life of ours. I mean, knowing how to bisect a sheep's eye is dead handy.'

'Not to sheep, it's not.' Brian smiled, 'All you end up with are moors full of one-eyed sheep wearing eye patches. I bet they are always bumping into each other and stumbling over cliff edges to their doom.'

Enoch couldn't be bothered to argue and so remained silent. Besides, watching Alan wobbling and sweating on the bucket was far more interesting than discussing the relative merits of monoptic, grass-eating wool machines.

'How many have I done now,' Alan panted.

Herbert hadn't been counting for the last five minutes. He had become pre-occupied with three ants who were holding a conference around a tiny piece of sugar. 'Er . . . er . . . One hundred and thirty,' he lied.

'Flippin' 'eck,' Alan complained, 'Dun't time go slow when you're balancing on a bucket?'

'Yer.' Herbert replied absentmindedly as he resumed his ant-watching.

'Our school rabbit is in the family way.' Rosie giggled. 'Miss Fillibut told us so. She's mystified as to how it's happened. I mean, the school's only got one rabbit.'

Enoch said nothing, but cast his mind back to when he'd looked after the school rabbit during the Easter break. No wonder Brian's rabbit always seemed to be smiling when they collected it after their day's play on the bombed-site. Still, they had been company for each other before the school rabbit was placed back into solitary confinement in the nature study room.

'It could be a miracle,' Margaret said.

'Yes,' Enoch supported. 'That's it. It's a miracle. I shouldn't worry about it. God moves in mysterious ways.'

'Yes,' Brian agreed, 'There are some things best left alone.'

'Yes,' Enoch said, then looked at Brian with a knowing expression. Brian smiled, shrugged his shoulders, then continued to stare hard at Alan, trying to hypnotise him into falling off the bucket. Alan's out-stretched arms were aching, and the stone which he hadn't noticed in his wellington boot was now producing a throbbing pain under his heel.

Suddenly Rosie shouted, 'Oh, no. Buzzy is dying. Look!'

The exclamation made Alan falter. He fought to regain his balance but it was to no avail. With a frustrated groan he toppled from the championship bucket and cursed Rosie. 'You burke. You've ruined any chance of a world record,' he fumed. Rosie ignored him and continued peering into the jam jar with a concerned expression on her face.

'How many did I do?' Alan asked Herbert anxiously.

'Er . . . er . . . one hundred and . . . er, forty-nine. Hard luck, Alan. You nearly made it.'

Alan spun to face Rosie and glared at her. Rosie was stroking the side of the glass and watching the blue-bottle as it lay on its back, feebly kicking its legs in the air. 'Don't die, Buzzy. Don't die,' she cooed.

'It's bound to die.' Enoch sniffed.

'How do you know, Enoch Thompson?' Rosie snarled.

'Stands to reason. There's no holes in the lid. It's snuffikating.' Enoch replied, matter-of-factly.

'Oh,' Rosie exclaimed, her hate evaporating. 'What can I do for him?'

'Knock some holes in it, of course.' Enoch said.

'Thanks, Enoch. Thanks.' Rosie gushed. 'You are helpful to wild creatures.'

Enoch tilted his head and accepted the praise nonchalantly. 'That's alright, Rosie,' he said graciously.

Rosie quickly found a rusty nail and, using a half a house-brick, began to ventilate Buzzy's home. 'There we are, Buzzy,' she said quietly, 'Did your little Rosie forget to give you air? Naughty Rosie.'

'I'm sure she's barmy,' Alan said, 'There's something wrong with people that talk to flies and animals.'

'Ah! Look at his little blue chest going up and down,' Rosie said, ignoring Alan's remark 'That's it, Buzzy. You do your breathing exercises until you get your breath back. Take no notice of this lot of animal haters. Your Rosie loves you.'

Alan looked at Enoch and then rolled his eyes up into his head in a resigned expression. Enoch tutted in disgust.

'Why don't you get a proper pet instead of a daft little fly?' Herbert asked. 'You can't tame a fly or mek it come when you call.'

'I don't want a proper pet,' Rosie shot back, 'I like Buzzy. He's my pet. So there. And he does know his name. Don't you Buzzy?' Rosie tapped the jam jar. The fly buzzed. 'See.' she exclaimed.

Herbert sniffed and then turned to watch the ants arguing as to who had first claim on the sugar.

'He doesn't know his name,' Enoch sneered, 'He's just terrified.'

'No, he's not.' Rosie snapped.

'Listen,' Enoch said determinedly, 'If you was in a jam jar and a giant kepted knocking the glass and staring in with his big eyes, you'd buzz a bit, wouldn't you? That fly of yours is terrified. I bet if you took the lid off, whoosh, off it would zoom and make a bee-line, I mean a blue-bottle-line for the nearest dustbin.'

Rosie pursed her lips, closed her eyes, tossed her head in disdain, hugged Buzzy to her chest, and turned her back on Enoch.

'Harry Staniforth has got a pet frog,' Herbert informed the gang, 'He's always taking it for a hop. He's made a little collar and lead for it.'

'Frogs don't hop,' Barry commented 'They use both legs to jump with. That's not hopping, is it? Frogs jump, they don't hop.'

'Well whatever they do, it doesn't matter, does it?' Herbert flared.

'I don't suppose so,' Barry agreed, 'But they don't hop. They jump.'

Herbert returned to his ants and watched with interest as one of the three scuttled to one side, climbed a broken house-brick, peered over the edge, shouted Geronimo, and jumped down onto the other two who were struggling over the sugar. They scattered and the remaining ant casually picked up the sugar grain and carried it off. Herbert silently clapped the ant's craftiness and originality in securing ownership of the food, whilst the two dazed ants pondered their loss, and wondered why God had singled them out to suffer life's misfortunes.

A bombed-site mouse, unseen by the gang, gained the surface of the ruins, observed the two-legged giants, sniffed the evening air, judged it was safe to make the short dash, and shot under Alan's world championship bucket.

High overhead, a bedraggled starling, feeling rather poorly due to a recent attack of asthma, winged its weary way towards its night-time roost amongst the sulphur-polluted air of the steelworks. It stopped beating its wings for a few seconds, gave a delicate cough, watched Barry wipe his hair in disgust, smirked, praised itself that in the midst of illness it could still aim straight, and continued its journey.

Margaret found herself a tiny forked stick and began hunting for spiders' webs amongst the ruins. Each time she found one she pushed the forked end into the centre, twiddled it, and collected the gossamer threads. As she worked she imagined she was a beautiful princess collecting silk to spin into cloth for her wedding dress in preparation for the day her Prince would come along and rescue her from her one-windowed tower. The spiders sat in their holes, cursing and swearing at the despoiler of geometric perfection, and wondering what the old man would say when he arrived home after a day of foraging and found the web missing.

'I'm going to have one last attempt on the world record,' Alan announced. He crossed to the bucket with a determined look on his face. 'What did you say the world record was?' he asked Herbert.

'Two hundred and twenty-two.' Herbert replied.

'Right,' Alan said, 'This is it.' He mounted the bucket, lifted one foot up, pushed his tongue out of the corner of his mouth, stretched his arms, and began his assault on the bucket Olympics.

Margaret returned, brushing past Alan as she dropped into the hollow. 'Sorry,' she said airily as Alan lost his balance and fell to the ground.

'Burke,' Alan cursed. 'I'll have to start again now.' He re-mounted the bucket and glared at Margaret's bent back.

'Right. This is it,' Alan shouted, 'Are you lot watching?'

'Yes,' they all answered, without looking up.

'Right. Here I go now.' Once more Alan took up the pose of a one-legged scarecrow.

'Don't forget to count, Herbert, will you?' Alan shouted as an after-thought. Herbert nodded his bent head.

Sometime later, the thoughts of Alan on his bucket forgotten, the gang sat listening to Rosie expounding the virtue of reading *The Home Doctor* and finding all the references to naughty bits to enlighten their childhood, when Alan called, 'How many have I done, Herbert?'

Herbert looked across to Alan and was surprised to see him still balancing on the bucket. 'Er . . . er . . . four hundred and ten.'

'What?' Alan exclaimed. 'Wowee. Four hundred and ten! I've beaten the world record. Wowee.' He jumped down from his perch shouting with happiness. 'Four hundred and ten. I'm a world champion. Wow. I'm the best in the world.' Herbert sniffed with disinterest, then returned to Rosie's lecture.

'How about that, then?' Alan asked proudly, but no-one took any notice of him.

'I said, how about that then?' he repeated more firmly.

'How about what?' Enoch shouted.

'My world record.'

'What world record?'

'My one-legged bucket-standing record,' Alan replied, slightly crestfallen.

'What about it?'

'I beat the world record.' Alan exclaimed.

'So what?'

'So, I'm the world champion.'

'Oh,' Enoch said. 'Is that good?'

'Of course it's good,' Alan said indignantly.

'Oh,' Enoch said, then shook his head. 'I don't know. Some people are easily pleased.'

Alan stood fuming. 'At least I'm a world champion,' he retorted.

'What's he rattling on about?' Rosie said, annoyed at being interrupted during her lecture.

'Alan's a world champion.' Enoch said flatly.

'At what?' Rosie asked, then not waiting for a reply, continued her lecture.

'Something to do with standing on a bucket, he says.'

'On a one-legged bucket,' Alan exclaimed.

'That's rare,' Barry joined in.

'Yes. I know it is,' Alan enthused. 'But I did it.'

'No. Not your world record,' Barry replied, 'There's millions of them. I didn't mean your world record.'

'What did you mean then?' Alan asked with a puzzled expression.

'One-legged buckets. They're rare. You don't see many of them about. Come to think about it, I don't think I've ever seen a one-legged bucket. Now that would be a world record. A one-legged bucket.' Alan clenched his fists and his blood boiled as Barry continued smirking at him.

'And so you see,' Rosie was concluding, 'Reading *The Family Doctor* book can prepare you for all kinds of little incidents and accidents.'

'How about flying, one-legged, world-championship buckets?' Alan seethed as he threw the bucket at them. The gang scattered and the bucket clanked and rolled about the vacated lecture hollow.

The mouse blinked its eyes at the sudden light, twitched its nose, looked up at fuming Alan, sighed, and decided to have an early night away from the mayhem of the bombed-site.

All Saints' Day

❋ ❋

THE GANG sat around the blazing fire on the bombed-site and wrestled with the bonfire toffee which Rosie's mother had made for the occasion. 'It's not much fun having bonfire night in the middle of the day, is it?' Brian said. 'I wish the war was over, then we could have it at the proper time.'

'Yes,' Enoch mumbled through glued teeth. 'Hitler's got a lot to answer for, spoiling Guy Fawkes night for him. I mean, it's the one night of the year that he gets a chance to be remembered, and now along comes Hitler trying to pinch the limes from his lights. If good old Guy Fawkes was still alive, I bet I know who'd be in for a bomb under his house. Hitler. Whoosh. Bang. Bonfire night back to its proper time in the scheme of life's things.'

The gang agreed, then continued massaging aching jaws whilst sucking on the dripping greased, burnt toffee. Alan reached and threw a piece of old window frame onto the fire, effectively cutting off Rosie's chance of retrieving her charred potato. Rosie didn't notice. The gang continued to try and force their teeth apart, feet quietly soaking socks in hot, rubber-smelling wellingtons. Eventually they finished the toffee and turned their attention to the bag of parkin which Margaret had made that morning.

'It's a bit hard. I forgot to put the treacle in,' she apologised with pride. 'But it's ever so good for you, me mam sez.'

The gang's newly-strengthened jaws began to attack the squares of parkin.

'Do you like it?' Margaret asked eagerly.

The gang all nodded. Margaret swelled with pride. 'I wonder if good old Guy Fawkes invented parkin?' Herbert asked, giving visibility to his words in a shower of crumbs.

'Suppose so,' Margaret sprayed back. 'After all, I bet he needed some grub to eat whilst he was waiting his chance to blow up Palmy-mint.'

'I wonder why he tried to blow up Parniment,' Barry quizzed.

'He did it to stop unjust laws and things being passed,' Enoch informed him. 'He was a great upholder of peace and kindness and other things.'

'Well, blowing things up doesn't sound very peaceful or kind if you ask me,' Rosie sniffed.

'Listen,' Enoch said forcefully, 'You want to think before you start gobbing off.

I mean, if he hadn't had a go at righting wrongs and blowing things up, we wouldn't be sat here now in front of a good fire eating his toffee and parkin and enjoying ourselves all over the place.'

'That's true,' Alan supported.

Enoch continued with gathered confidence. 'We could do wiv a few more heroes like Guy Fawkes, couldn't we? I think he ought to be called Saint Guy, not just Guy Fawkes. Anybody that can cause us to have as much fun as this as got to be worth Sainting, hasn't he? That's the trouble with this world at large of ours. Not enough Saints. I mean. I only know of Saint Chris-too-far and, er, er, Sloppy Saint Val-ter-line.'

'What about Saint George?' Margaret asked.

'Oh yer, I forgot about him,' Enoch answered.

'And Saint Swithin.'

'Yer. Yer. Alright. Them as well,' Enoch said. 'But, I mean, that's not many is it? There must be room for tons more Saints.'

'Such as?' Rosie sneered.

'Well, er, Saint . . . Saint . . . Saint . . . Saint Dick', Enoch said triumphantly.

'Saint who?' Barry giggled.

'Saint Dick,' Enoch repeated.

'Which one is he?' Brian asked.

'Saint Dick Turpin,' Enoch replied. 'I mean, he'd mek a great Saint, wouldn't he? And he's from around here.'

'I didn't know that,' Alan exclaimed.

'Oh yes,' Enoch said. 'He's a local 'un is Dick Turpin. He was always riding this way when he was holding stage-coaches up and pinching kisses off the women passengers. And what about him breaking the world record for riding his horse, Black Beauty, from London. That deserves a Sainting if anything does. I think we ought to have a Saint Dick Day every year.'

'Well, we couldn't have a bonfire to celebrate him wiv,' Herbert said. 'That's special to Guy Fawkes is that.'

'Yer, I know that. But we could have . . . er . . . er . . . games, and tricks and . . . er . . . other things. We could even have a fancy dress competition and prizes for the best dressed Dick.'

'The mind boggles,' Rosie said quietly. Brian giggled.

'What about Robin Hood then?' Herbert said. 'I think he deserves a Sainting, probably more than Saint Dick. Don't forget he was always robbing from the poor and giving to the rich.'

'You've got it the wrong way round,' Enoch said good naturedly. 'You mean robbing from the rich and giving to the poor.'

'Well, there you are then,' Herbert defended. 'If he did it that way round, he deserves to be a Saint even more. Doesn't he?'

'That's true,' Alan supported.

'You're right, Herbert,' Enoch said. 'Saint Robin. That sounds real good. Saint Robin.'

'And it describes what his job was in this life of ours,' Alan added. 'I mean. Saint Robin. That's what he did for a living, isn't it, robbing? It's a perfect name is that.'

Everyone was in agreement.

'What could we do on Saint Robin's day?' Barry asked, as he prodded at his personal potato in the fire.

'We could have bow and arrow contests, and, er, eating contests, and carving wood competitions under the greenwood trees,' Herbert offered.

'There's not many greenwood trees around here,' Rosie sniffed.

'We could pretend,' Enoch said defiantly.

The gang grew quiet and stared into the flames, each one thinking of new Saints to canonise. Every so often each one would name a new Saint out loud and the others guessed which person had been favoured. 'Saint Roy . . . Roy Rogers. Saint Winston . . . Winston Churchill. Saint Long . . . Long John Silver,' until they ran out of names, and sat quietly once more. The wood on the fire continued to periodically crackle and explode, throwing showers of sparks into the evening air. Their eyes became heavy with the heat and their mouths grew dry. Alan reached, and unscrewing the stopper from a pop bottle, he took a deep drink of water, then handed the bottle around.

'I bet this is just how cowboys feel after a day on the prairie,' Herbert said quietly.

Immediately the bombed-site faded from their minds and vast, grass waving vistas appeared. A herd of steers chewed contentedly some distance away. Enoch reached into his pocket and withdrew his fluff-covered mouth organ. He put it to his lips, and drawing a deep breath, began to play the plaintive notes of 'Yes, we have no bananas.' It jarred somewhat, but no-one complained.

'The steers are a bit restless tonight,' Brian said.

'What do you mean?' Margaret asked, puzzled.

'I'm playing at being a cowboy,' Brian explained.

'Oh,' Margaret said.

'Yes. I've noticed that,' Alan agreed, joining the fantasy. 'I expect it's because we've been punching them all day.'

'We don't punch cows . . . We poke them. That's why we're called cowpokes,' Enoch said as he stopped playing and banged the spit from the mouth organ onto

Rosie's discarded cardigan. 'We're called cow punches as well,' Alan answered. 'I read it in my Buffalo Bill Wild West Annual.'

'Oh,' Enoch said, and began playing *Silent Night*.

'That's bad luck is that,' Rosie informed Enoch.

'What is?'

'Playing carols when it's not Christmas.'

Enoch changed tune and began playing *Little Brown Jug*.

'I think I'll go and brand a few heads,' Herbert said and standing, withdrew a burning length of wood from the fire. He left the hollow and then returned some minutes later. Alan looked up and affecting a cowboy accent asked, 'How did the branding go, partner?'

'Alright, partner,' Herbert answered, 'Although one of the cows was a bit awkward. I had to poke it a few times to stop it mooing all over the place. And then I gave it a good punching. It's quiet now.' He sat on his house-brick and asked, 'How's about some coffee, partner?'

'We haven't got any,' answered Rosie, the self-appointed chuck-wagon cook.

'Well how's about some apple-jack?'

'We're right out,' Rosie replied.

'Flippin' 'eck, partner. This is a rubbish cattle drive I've joined. I think I'll give me notice in and join another one tomorrow.'

'I've got some prairie strawberries,' Rosie said helpfully.

'What's them?' Herbert queried.

'Beans,' Rosie replied. 'That's what cowboys and cowgirls call beans. Prairie strawberries.'

'Right,' Herbert said, 'I'll have some of them, then.'

Rosie passed an invisible plate to Herbert and he began eating the imaginary food. 'Mighty fine. Mighty fine,' he muttered.

'You want to be careful eating all them prairie beans,' Alan warned. 'You know what they do to your stomach. You could cause a right stampede, partner.'

'Yes,' Barry added, 'It would be just like that film we saw last week. *Gone With The Wind*.

Enoch chuckled through the mouth organ, then the Little Brown Jug shattered into laughter.

'That's it. Go on. Spoil the game!' Rosie exclaimed icily. 'You lot always have to spoil everything.'

'I've just thought of another one,' Alan said.

'Another what?' Enoch asked as he continued to chuckle.

'Another Saint.'

'Who?' Herbert queried.

'Saint Pokey,' Alan answered. 'Saint Pokey. He could be the patron saint of cowboys.'

'What about Saint Punchy as well?' Brian added.

'Yer,' Alan said. 'Punchy and Pokey. Saints of all the world's cowboys.'

'And cowgirls,' Margaret added.

'Alright,' Alan conceded, 'Them as well. They could ride the range on their heavenly horses, protecting cowboys . . . '

'And cowgirls,' Margaret persisted.

'From dangerous bullets and outlaws,' Alan glared at Margaret.

'Yes,' Enoch joined in. 'There could be a special Punchy and Pokey day, and all the cowboys . . . '

'And cowgirls,' Margaret interjected.

'Could celebrate and go around punching and poking steers and cattle. They could even have special poking competitions. And the cowboys . . . '

'And cowgirls,' Margaret said.

Enoch turned, and through narrowed eyes gave her a silent warning.

'And the cowboys,' Enoch emphasised. Margaret made to add her piece, but thought better of it, deciding that discretion was the better part of valour.

'And the cowboys could poke any cowgirls that didn't know their proper place around the camp fire,' he finished menacingly. He turned from Margaret. She stuck her tongue out at his back.

'Well, I don't know how you could mek all them people Saints,' Rosie said scornfully. 'It's not our job to make Saints anyway. It's the church's job is that.'

'Yes,' Enoch said after some moments thought. 'But somebody as to tell the church who they think would make a good un. Don't they? After all, you can't expect vicars to know everything all the time. I bet they have to rely on the man who's common to tell them.' Suddenly that divine spark of intervention struck Enoch between the eyes. He had an idea.

'I know!' he exclaimed excitedly. 'Why don't we write a list of people we think should be Saints? We could then give it to Mr. Friez and he could pass it on to God for his say-so. I bet Mr. Friez would be dead grateful to be able to do something for God for a change. Instead of always asking him to forgive him.'

'That's a smashing idea,' Alan supported. 'Who's got a pencil?'

Soon they were all calling various nominations for Sainthood to a busy, tongue-chewing Enoch, who scrawled the names onto the back of the brown paper bag. Eventually he stopped writing, not because the list was exhausted, but for the simple reason that the paper was now covered in names both local and exotic.

'I think we've got enough,' he announced proudly.

'What now?' Rosie asked.

'We deliver the list. Come on.'

The gang stood, and throwing vast amounts of wood onto the fire to ensure it's continued health during their absence, they crossed the bombed-site towards the twinkling lights of the vicarage.

'You knock,' Rosie hissed.

'I'm not,' Alan exclaimed.

'Coward,' Brian said.

The gang all stood at the bottom of the privet hedged path facing a solid, carved door which was set in an equally stout stone architrave.

'I'll do it,' Enoch said positively. He reached and knocked on the door. They waited some minutes. Nothing.

'Perhaps no-one's in,' Margaret whispered.

'Of course there is. All the lights are on,' Enoch said firmly. 'It's a big house, don't forget. Perhaps they didn't hear me knock. I need something to bang harder with.' He looked around and spotted a hand-sized stone under the privet. 'This will do,' he said, and straightening, smashed the rock repeatedly against the door. 'I bet they've heard that,' he whispered.

'I should think every house in the street heard that,' Rosie mumbled.

From the far side of the door they heard footsteps. 'Someone's coming,' Brian hissed. Instinctively they all huddled closer together. There was the sound of a bolt being drawn and a key turning in the lock.

'It's just like that ghost story on the wireless, isn't it?' Barry quavered. The gang shivered.

The door swung slowly open and light spilled onto them. Mr. Friez, the vicar, stood looking down at them. His face broke into a kindly smile. 'Hello, children,' he said gently. 'Was it you knocking?'

Enoch secretly dropped the stone into the soft earth and answered, 'Yes, Mr. Friez.'

'Well now. What can I do for you?'

Rosie nudged Enoch in the back.

'I know. I know. Stop pushing,' Enoch flared. 'Er, Mr. Friez, we've brought you this.' He held out the list of candidates for Sainthood and then in a gush of words, explained to the holy man their idea, finishing with, 'And so we thought you could have a word with God to see if it was alright.'

Mr. Friez glanced at the list and noted all the local names which were written there. With a manner born of a deep love and understanding of children, he raised his head and looked at the dirty upturned, eager faces. 'Do you know, children, I think this is a lovely idea. I'm sure that when I talk with God tonight he will agree. Perhaps before you all go to sleep tonight, you too could pray to him. You never know, he might tell you his decision then. Will you do that?'

The gang all nodded their heads vigorously.

'God bless, children,' Mr. Friez said, and made the sign of the cross over them.

The gang stood until the door closed, then they turned and ran back to their blazing bonfire in the distance.

The sky grew dark as evening gave way to twilight. Stars began to appear and shimmered in the heat of the fire. 'I hope all them around here are grateful when they become Saints,' Enoch said, 'I hope they remember who it was that put their names forward for a Sainting.'

'Yer,' the gang all chorused through mouths full of roast potato.

Suddenly from the lip of the hollow an adult voice boomed.

'And what do you lot think you're doing? Don't you know there's a bloody war on?'

They all jumped, then spun round to face Mr. Lindley. He stood with a tin hat on his head, an ARP armband around his coat sleeve, and a bucket and stirrup pump in his hands.

'Put that bloody fire out, you little buggers. Bombers could see that blaze from miles up.' He placed the bucket to the ground, fitted the stirrup pump, and began dowsing the fire. The gang stared at him with open mouths, then watched as he took great delight in extinguishing Saint Guy's Fire. Soon all that was left was a smouldering heap of soggy wood.

'And let that be a lesson to you, you little sods,' he oathed, then turning, he disappeared over the bombed-site.

Enoch stared after him, then looked at their ruined pleasure.

'Right,' he breathed fiercely. 'I know where I'm going first thing tomorrow. I'm going to the vicarage. His name is coming straight off the Sainting list. In fact, I'll not wait until tomorrow. I'll have a word with God tonight about this.'

And the gang supported him.

Nelson

A LAN lay on the bombed-site surrounded by the rest of the gang. His eyes stared wildly at the sky, his limbs jerked in exaggerated spasms and he groaned loudly. 'Will he die?' Rosie asked Doctor Enoch.

'Fraid so. He's got a cannon ball wedged in his heart.'

'Is that fatal?' Midshipman Brian enquired, 'Couldn't you otterate and remove it?'

'I haven't got my otterating tools anymore,' the good doctor replied, 'They were blown away during the battle.'

'You could use my dagger,' Bosun Herbert offered eagerly.

Doctor Enoch ignored Herbert and knelt at the side of their dying hero. Alan raised himself up onto one elbow and gasped, 'Before I die, will you kiss me, Hardy?'

'Don't be sloppy,' Enoch sneered, 'Us doctors don't go around kissing our patients every time they are dying. You're supposed to be a famous Captain. You should know better. I mean, us Britishers don't go around kissing each other. We're supposed to be tough and strong. Now get on with your dying.'

'Farewell my trusted crew of the fag ship Victory. You fought a good battle for me against them French,' Alan breathed. 'Don't forget to build a big column for me in London and put me on top.'

'The wind will blow you off,' Margaret informed Nelson.

'No, not me. I didn't mean me, as in me. I meant a statue of me.'

'Oh,' Margaret said. 'Do you want a statue wiv your hat on or off?' Barry asked.

'On,' Alan replied.

'Do you want to be standing or sitting?'

'Standing, of course,' Alan answered.

'Do you want your patch over your eye which you have lost?'

'Of course I do,' Alan said with a note of irritability creeping in.

'Do you want both arms on, or just the one?'

'I've only got one arm, burke. Now shut up and let me die.' Alan resumed the posture of Britain's dying hero. 'When I'm dead,' he sighed, 'If you find out that England is in any trouble at any time, just bang my famous drum and I'll come running to save you all.'

'How will you get down from the top of your column?' Enoch asked, 'It will be a big jump. You might kill yourself again, my Captain.'

Suddenly Rosie said, 'Nelson didn't have a drum. It was that other famous Captain who used to play with his balls on the cliffs down south. They called him Francis Drake. He had a famous drum.'

'Well, bang his then,' Nelson Alan snapped, 'I mean, it doesn't matter whose drum you bang, just as long as I can hear it in heaven.'

'What code shall we use?' Herbert asked.

'What do you mean, what code shall you use?'

'I mean, how many bangs shall we do to call you?'

Alan thought for a moment, then said, 'Do two for a small danger, three for a big one, and four if all the world is in trouble.'

'What if Francis Drake won't lend us his drum?' Brian asked.

'Tell him it's the famous Nelson who needs it,' Alan replied, 'He knows me. I taught him how to sail a boat and how to play with his balls properly. We're friends.'

'Right-ho,' Brian answered.

'Which way do you want to face?' Barry asked Alan.

'What do you mean?' Nelson asked.

'Which way do you want to face when you're up your column?'

'Oh, I don't know,' Alan sighed in exasperation. 'Face me towards the sea so that I can see my faithful ship, the Victory, for the rest of my days.'

'You won't be able to see it at night,' Herbert informed the weary hero.

'Or when it's foggy,' Rosie added.

'He could if he took a bright light and his telescope up the column with him,' Brian offered helpfully.

'Oh yes,' Herbert said, 'I hadn't thought of that.'

'Right,' Nelson said fiercely, 'If you lot have finished, can I get on with my dying?'

'Yes,' Herbert said placidly.

'Right. Where was I?' Nelson pondered, 'Oh yes. Yes, good sailors of mine, I will come every time you bang the drum. I will save you all from troublesome times and other things. I am dying now. Oh, oh. The cannon ball. It weighs a ton. It is pressing the life out of my bodyliness. I am dying. Ah, ah. When I am dead dig a big hole for me and bury me at sea in David Jones lock-up.'

Nelson Alan sighed, closed one eye, and was no more.

Margaret, who up to this point had remained silent, suddenly cried out, 'Nelson is dead. England has lost a famous son. Gone to a grave full of water. Will we never see the like of him again? This hero of all England, this famous Captain, this man who saved our country. Who will run ashore and break this rotten news to the rest of England's people?'

'We could toss up for it,' Doctor Enoch offered.

'I'm not tossing up with you Enoch Thompson. I know you. You cheat,' Margaret exclaimed.

'No I don't,' Enoch said.

'Yes you do,' Margaret glared, 'You use a double-headed penny. I've seen it.'

Enoch smirked. 'OK, Margaret. You can go and tell everybody then,' he conceded.

'Right, if that's sorted out, can we get on with giving Nelson a burial at sea?' Rosie asked.

The gang pushed and pulled until Nelson Alan was finally stretched out on a piece of rough floor-boarding which was balanced on the lip of their favourite hollow. Barry stepped forward and reverently threw a potato sack over him.

'Farewell, oh son of all Merry England,' Enoch shouted, and together with Barry lifted the floor-boarding up, tilting it down into the hole. Nelson Alan slipped from under the sacking and slid down the length of wood. Suddenly there was a terrific yell as Alan fell into the hollow clutching his backside.

'Bloody 'eck ,' he shouted, his face twisted in pain. 'Me bum's full of splinters.'

Enoch and Barry collapsed to the ground roaring with laughter as Nelson continued to clutch at his bottom. 'Good job you decided to stand on your column and not sit,' Barry howled.

'At this rate, there'll be hardly anything left of him to put up there,' Enoch choked.

Rosie jumped down into the hollow and asked eagerly, 'Would you like me to look at your bum and pull the spells out, Alan?'

'Gerroff,' Nelson menaced. 'I'm going home. It's not funny, you know.'

*   *   *   *

Sometime later, the game over, the gang sat on the vicarage wall watching with interest as the bailiffs repossessed Mr. Wheelstone's radiogram and loaded it into a plain van. Mrs. Wheelstone stood with a worried expression on her face, wondering how she would explain her misuse of the weekly payments to her quick-tempered husband. Eventually the van pulled away. Mrs. Wheelstone glanced up and down the street, checking which neighbours had seen the shameful scene. She saw Mrs. Brigham's ample backside hanging over the upstairs window sill, as she polished away at the glass, and realised she had witnessed everything in the reflection. She gave a false laugh and shouted up,

'The bloody thing's broken again. It's gone to the menders.'

Mrs. Brigham smirked knowingly and watched as Mrs. Wheelstone's face slipped back to its worried expression as she disappeared down her entry, back to the anonymity of her kitchen. Mrs. Brigham resumed her window cleaning with renewed vigour and a happy heart full of newly acquired, virgin, gossip.

'I wonder if that's where that sailors expression comes from?' Enoch said as his eyes drifted to Mrs. Brigham's rear view.

'What saying?' Rosie enquired.

'That saying they were always using on Nelson's ship.'

'What was that?' Brian asked.

'You know. A vast behind,'

Enoch chuckled. The rest of the gang laughed quietly, all that is except Alan, who stood by the wall with no desire to sit.

'They have some funny sayings, don't they. Sailors, I mean,' Herbert said, 'You know. Like shivering timbers, and yard arms, and kipper the halyards. And they are always spicing a man's braces, aren't they?'

'Yes,' Enoch agreed, 'It must take months to learn about a big ship before you're allowed to drive one on the open road.'

'And they have to get used to being sea-sick all over the place as well,' Barry added.

'Our sailors are never sea-sick,' Enoch exclaimed indignantly, 'We're British. British sailors are never sea-sick. French sailors are. But not British sailors. We're too tough.'

'The French don't call it sea-sick,' Rosie said knowledgeably, 'They call it *mal de mare*. That's French for sea-sick is that.'

'Hark at her,' Enoch sneered, '*Mal de mare*. Lah de dah.'

'Well, they do,' Rosie answered sullenly.

'Where did you learn that from. Off a sauce bottle?' Herbert laughed.

No, I didn't,' Rosie said archly, 'I've got an English to French dictionary what my mam got from my dead uncle Jack. It's full of useful sayings like that. So there.'

'Useful. What's useful about that?' Enoch demanded.

Rosie fought for an answer and found one. 'It stops you being ignorant like what you are, Enoch Thompson,' she spat out.

Enoch's mouth tightened and his eyes narrowed with hate whilst the rest of the gang laughed along with Rosie. Eventually they calmed and sat quietly, letting their eyes wander at will around their familiar domain.

'The gas-lamp man is coming,' Brian observed as he watched the distant figure on his bicycle pedalling up the road. All eyes swung in his direction, and as he approached their personal gas-lamp they watched with familiar interest.

'How many turns?' Enoch asked.

'Six,' Rosie said.

'Five,' Alan spoke.

'Eight,' Barry added.

'I'll say seven,' Enoch stated. The one-armed man swung his short ladder to the cross arms of the lamp and with a nimbleness born of hundreds of such actions each week, climbed to the head of the lamp. The gang watched keenly as he opened the clockwork case under the lamp and began winding the timer mechanism.

'Eight,' Barry breathed, 'I win.'

'You were lucky,' Brian said grudgingly.

Barry sat smiling at his small victory. 'Do you know,' Enoch said thoughtfully, 'I bet that's just how Captain Nelson looked when he used to climb up his rigging to look for French ships.'

'Yes,' the gang breathed as they continued watching the one-armed gas man cleaning the tiny windows of the lamp head.

'If he'd got an eye-patch he'd be Nelson's double,' Margaret said quietly.

'What's he doing now?' Rosie asked. 'He's fitting a new mantle,' Brian informed her. They watched as the gas man struck a match and flared off the delicate glue which protected the gossamer threads of the fragile mantle. Closing the glass door, he descended the ladder, pulled it free of the cross arms, hooked it along the bicycle, swung his leg over the saddle, grasped the handle-bars centrally, and after a few seconds of wobbling, pedalled away from the kerb towards his next beacon of comfort.

'He's clever,' Rosie said as the bicycle disappeared around the top of the street, 'For a one-armed man, he's dead clever, and he's a smashing balancer.'

They agreed, with the exception of Enoch. He sniffed and said, 'Not half as clever as Nelson. Nelson could steer a whole ship and win battles as well. And it's harder balancing on a ship's deck in a gale than it is just riding a one-armed bike. And don't forget, Nelson only had one eye.'

'Well, yes,' Alan said, 'I suppose so. But don't forget, Nelson was a hero. Doing things like that is easy for a hero. I mean, the gas-lamp man is just ordinary, isn't he?'

'He might just be ordinary,' Rosie defended, 'But he's just as clever at his job as what Nelson was at his. I expect that if the gas man had had a chance of having a big ship, well, no doubt he'd be a hero by now.'

'And,' Margaret supported, 'The gas man would be better than Nelson when England was in trouble, wouldn't he?'

'Why,' Enoch asked, puzzled.

'Well, he's used to climbing up and down ladders, isn't he? He'd be able to run up and down his column all day saving England with no trouble at all.'

'And no doubt he'd have his own gas-lamp up there to see with at night,' Rosie supported.

Enoch sighed, set his face in a resigned expression, and said quietly, 'I don't know. You lot make me feel *mal de mared*.'

Magical Childhood

'**M**Y MOTHER is always putting things in a safe place,' Herbert said, as he watched Enoch trying to pluck up enough courage to swallow the wooden sword he had made. 'She always says the same thing. "I'll just put this in a safe place so I'll know where it is". Our house is full of safe places that she can't find. And she always accuses us of having moved whatever it is she's put in a safe place and can't find!'

'Yesterday it was two rubber suspender buttons. She turned the house upside down looking for them. Mind you, she found the milk checks that she'd put in a safe place a month ago. But no suspender buttons.'

'Perhaps,' Rosie said, 'If she'd looked for the milk checks instead of the suspender buttons, she'd have found the suspender buttons and not the milk checks.'

'I never thought of that,' Herbert replied.

Rosie swelled with pride. 'There's more in my head than nits,' she answered.

Yes,' Alan said quietly, 'There's dicks and bugs and bird's nests.' Rosie turned and glared across at Alan who was busy nailing wood together in an attempt to make a magic box that would produce snow-white doves.

'You two will never be magicians,' she sneered, 'You don't know any magic.'

'Listen, clever clogs,' Alan replied, 'All we need is the right tackle. Once that's made, magicking is easy. I mean. Look at my partner, Enoch. He's made his sword. That was the hard part. Now all he's got to do is to swallow it. Dead easy is that.'

'It's taking him some time,' Margaret sniffed, 'He's been at it half-an-hour, and so far he's made every excuse there is and only managed to get an inch in his gob.'

'That's a lie,' Enoch exclaimed, and regretted doing so immediately. The tip of his sword caught his left nostril. Clutching his nose, and squeezing tears from his eyes, he went on, 'Talking to magicians like what I am whilst I'm doing a deaf-defying trick could cause instant deaf to us old troupers.'

'Yes,' Alan supported, 'Us stage persons need absolute calm whilst we are magicking about all over the place.'

Margaret sniffed again and muttered, 'You're both crackers.'

'You'll see how crackers we are when we're appearing at the world-famous

Attercliffe Palace twice a night and getting paid tons of money to disappear.'

'Disappearing is the best thing that could happen to you two burkes,' Rosie answered.

'You'll see,' Alan said, then continued knocking a bent, rusty nail, into the soggy piece of floorboard.

'Well, magicking doves and swallowing swords won't get you far in this life of ours,' Margaret replied.

'That's not all we do,' Enoch exclaimed, 'We're going to have a brain-reading act as well, aren't we, Alan? We'll become known as the great brain readers of Britain. We'll know everything that people are thinking.'

'Yes,' Alan supported, 'So put that in your pipe and smoke it.' ,

'Go on, then,' Rosie challenged, 'What am I thinking now?' She screwed her face up and squeezed her eyes shut.

'Sorry. We can't read your brain, Rosie,' Enoch smirked, 'Don't forget, Miss Fillibut said you hadn't got a thought in your head.'

Alan laughed. 'Well, read mine then,' Margaret said defiantly

'Er . . . alright,' Alan said. Enoch looked across at him with ill-concealed surprise. Alan held his hand to his head, shut his eyes, and after a few moments said, in a far-away voice, 'You are thinking about your dinner.'

'No, I'm not,' Margaret sneered, 'I was thinking about Mrs. Brigham's chickens.'

'You're lying,' Alan exclaimed, looking around for support, 'You've just changed your mind to make me look daft. She's lying.'

'That's true,' Enoch said matter of factly, 'I got the same message. I saw a big plate of stew and Margaret eating it.'

'They're both lying,' Margaret said indignantly.

'Prove it!' said Alan. Margaret knew this was impossible and began to sulk.

'He does magic,' Brian informed the gang.

'Who?' Barry asked.

'Mr. Lindley. He does magic. He's got a top hat and tails. He does shows for the spanner-maker's institute and the home for wayward women. My dad says he's always up to his tricks down there.'

'Is he any good at it?' Enoch enquired with a fellow-professional's interest.

'Don't know,' Brian replied, 'But he's made a magic disappearing cabinet in his bedroom. He was at it for two weeks. He nearly sent me dad barmy when he was on nights.'

'Well, I've never seen him with a magic cabinet,' Alan sniffed.

'No. And you won't,' Brian replied, 'When he'd built it he found it was too big. He couldn't get it out of his bedroom. He uses it as a wardrobe now.'

Enoch thought for a moment, then remarked, 'Well, if he was any good at magicking, like what I am, he'd have magicked it out of his bedroom with no problem at all. Dead easy is that.'

Rosie gave Enoch a sideways look that spoke volumes.

'What are you two going to call yourselves?' Herbert enquired.

Both Alan and Enoch thought hard then Alan said, 'The two Magical Mesters of Mystery and Clever Tricks.'

'They'll never get that lot on a poster,' Rosie objected, 'There won't be any room for the other act's names.'

'That's their problem,' Enoch said, 'Besides, when we're appearing there won't be any other acts. We'll be too good. We'll take up all of the show. We're not sharing our money with tap dancers and jugglers and sloppy singers.'

'Too true,' Alan agreed, 'Let them make their own way in life. It costs a lot of money to buy tricks from the joke shop. All that lot do is bang their feet on the ground and throw wood at each other and sing with their gobs. They don't spend money on their acts. Not like me and Enoch. I mean, a top hat with tails on it costs a bob or two for a start. And there's always rabbits to buy. They don't last forever, you know. They soon wear out. And there's always doves to buy. I mean, given half a chance they're always buggering off, aren't they?'

Enoch nodded wisely then said, 'And we'll need a tin of polish.'

'What for?' Alan asked his partner.

'To smarten up the act and to keep my sword bright, of course.'

'It's made of wood,' Margaret observed.

'Yes. *This* one's made of wood. I know that. But this is only my practice sword. My *real* one will be made of steel. It's a well-known fact of us sword swallowers, that our swords are made of real steel. If you was on the stage like what we is, you'd know that.'

'Hark at him,' Rosie exclaimed, 'It will cost a pound to talk to him soon. Excuse me your highness, can I have your autograph?'

Enoch put his tongue out at her, then, turning away, threw his head back, and resumed his wood swallowing practice.

'Well I'm not sitting around here all day watching these two burkes messing about. I'm going to play in the den,' Rosie said. 'Are you coming, Margaret?'

Margaret nodded and the two girls wandered away to the distant ruins.

'I'm glad they've gone,' Enoch said, 'They were putting me off my work.'

'Yes,' Alan agreed,' Perhaps we can get on with it now. How's your sword swallowing coming along?'

'Great,' Enoch enthused, 'I got it down to the handle a minute ago. It was when you were busy making your smashing magic box.'

'I didn't see you,' Herbert spoke.

'Well, no, you wouldn't. You weren't looking, that's why. And you can't expect me to shout, "Look at me, everybody. Look what I've done." Not with a mouth full of sword. That would be dangerous. I'd end up cutting my head off, wouldn't I?'

Herbert said nothing, but sniffed in disbelief.

'I think I'll have a rest from sword swallowing and get on with making my famous collapsing bird cage,' Enoch announced. From a dirty potato sack he fished out an equally dirty chip pan basket.

'What's that trick do?' Barry enquired.

'Oh, this,' Enoch said, holding up the greasy basket. 'This is the best trick of all what I do.' Alan looked at him accusingly,

'What *we* do,' Enoch corrected, 'What we do is to fill this magic birdcage up to the top with budgies. Then my partner puts a cloth over it and then I push a million swords though the cloth and then set fire to it, whilst Alan bashes the cage to bits with a sledge hammer and I plug it into the lights and throw it into a bucket of water.'

'There must be easier ways to kill budgies,' Herbert said sarcastically.

'That's the trick,' Enoch exclaimed, 'It doesn't kill them. It's magic. They just disappear and then appear out of Alan's top hat with tails. It's the last trick in our act. It will cause the building to fall down with clapping.'

'I don't believe you two will be able to do that trick,' Barry protested. 'For a start, where would you find all them budgies? Budgies cost a lot of money, you know.'

'Ah. That's where you're wrong. We've thought of that. We're going to buy budgie eggs and hatch them ourselves. Aren't we, Alan?' Enoch said. Alan nodded his head unconvincingly.

'Shops don't sell budgie eggs,' Herbert spoke.

'We won't get them from the shops. 'We'll get them from, er . . . Mrs. Lindley.'

'She doesn't sell budgie eggs,' Barry said.

'No. I know that. But she's got a budgie. I'll ask her to ask Billie to lay us a couple of dozen. I mean, he's got plenty of time on his hands.'

'Claws,' Alan corrected.

'Oh yer. Claws,' Enoch said, 'I mean, all he does all day is bash his bell and wear his little ladder out. I bet he'd be glad to have a real job for a change. It shouldn't take him long to conjure up some eggs for us.'

'Can Billie do tricks, then?' Herbert asked.

'What do you mean?'

'Well, you said Billie can conjure up eggs.'

'Burke!' Enoch snapped.

'How are you going to hatch them?' Barry enquired.

Enoch thought for a moment then said, 'Me and Alan are going to have turns and take them to bed with us every night until they are borned. After that we will have more budgies than we know what to do with.'

'I think Margaret is right. You're both crackers,' Barry said quietly, 'I'm going to the den to play. Are you coming, Herbert?'

Herbert nodded and they crossed the ruins towards the bombed church, leaving the two masters of magic to dream of fame and fortune.

Sometime later Enoch announced, 'There we are. The magic cage is finished.' He held the chip basket up for Alan to admire. 'Well, that's all the tricks made,' Alan said, 'What now?'

'Tomorrow, Enoch said grandly, 'Tomorrow we'll go down to the *Attercliffe Palace* and join the theatre. Then, after that we'll go on a world tour all over England.'

'Oh,' Alan said with a sudden pang of homesickness, 'What about school?'

'Famous magicians don't go to school,' Enoch exclaimed.

'Oh,' Alan said, 'Well, what are we going to do for the rest of today?'

Enoch thought for a moment then said, 'Let's go and join the others in the den for a farewell play.'

Alan's face broke into a sunshine smile and he said eagerly, 'Yes. That will be great,' and together they ran over the broken bricks and rubble towards the magic of childhood.

Heads You Win,
Legs You Lose

* *

'I WONDER what we'll be when we grow up?' Rosie asked as she carefully finished buttoning the hand-knitted cardigan around her chipped, black doll and smoothed it maternally with her hand.

'Big,' Brian answered.

'No. I didn't mean that,' Rosie replied, 'I mean I wonder what we will do? You know. Jobs and things.'

'Don't know,' Brian said. 'Growing up is millions of miles away. I don't think we'll ever get there. I bet we spend all our lifeness trying to get to being grown-up. And when we are, if we ever are, I bet it feels just the same as what it does now, except there will be more rules and things to obey.'

'Too true,' said Enoch wisely, 'Being grown-up just means wearing bigger clothes and eating bigger meals and er, bossing about them that's on their way to growing up.'

'Suppose so,' Rosie agreed, 'Still, grown-ups seem to be allowed to do a lot more things than what we are. Look at Mr. Dent. He spends all his time sitting in his garden writing.'

'Hah, yes,' Enoch replied, 'But Mr. Dent has stopped working on account of his old ageness and his lost leg. And anyway, he doesn't just write, as in letters. He writes stories and books. He's a nauthor. That's special, is that. I mean, how many people do you know who nauthor about for a living?'

'I've never seen any of his books,' Alan spoke. 'There's none of his books at our school. He can't make much money from writing if his books aren't on our school shelves.'

'Perhaps he keeps all the books he writes. I mean, Mr. Carr makes ships in bottles, doesn't he? But he doesn't sell them or give them to schools, does he?' Barry commented. 'You should see his house. You can't move for ships in bottles. He's got them everywhere. A whole house full of ships in bottles. He's doing a special one now. He calls it his piece of resistance. It's a massive galleon. He's going to fit it into a milk churn.'

'That's daft!' Enoch exclaimed. 'You can't see through a steel milk churn.'

'I know,' Barry agreed, 'But that's the clever part. He's going to call it The Ghostly Galleon of Captain Blood inside Fingal's Cave. You'll only be able to see it when he takes the lid off and shines his torch in. My dad says you've got to hand it to him. He says he's got tons of patience, spending his life half-way inside a milk churn building a boat.'

'He got stuck last week,' Brian said casually. 'Mrs. Carr had to send for the fire brigade to free him. He was stuck inside for three hours.'

'Fancy,' Margaret said quietly, 'That could have been very dangerous. What if the tide had come in? Drowned in a milk churn, miles from the sea.'

Rosie chuckled.

'How did they get him out?' Herbert asked.

'The brave fire-fighters greased his head and out he popped covered in glue and string,' Barry explained. 'Mrs. Carr didn't half play hell with him afterwards. I mean, you know how firemen can guzzle tea. She had to borrow a packet from Mrs. Brigham. And they ate all her scones. It took her two hours to get rid of them, what with them lounging about in her kitchen and guzzling her tea and scones. I mean. Half the town could have burned down, couldn't it? And where were the firemen? In Mrs. Carr's having a party.'

'Disgustable,' Margaret said.

'Yer. Flippin' double disgustable,' Herbert supported, 'It's a wonder Mr. Carr didn't play hell with them for neglecting their duty.'

'He wasn't bothered,' Barry explained. 'He'd climbed back into his milk churn with two new masts.'

'That shows a great dedication to duty, does that,' Rosie breathed. 'The firemen could do with taking a leaf out of Mr. Carr's book, couldn't they?'

'No,' Enoch said, 'Mr. Carr doesn't write books. It's one-legged Mr. Dent who writes books. Mr. Carr builds ships.'

Rosie looked at Enoch and shook her head in a pitying gesture.

'I wonder what he writes about when he's all alone in his garden?' Margaret asked.

'Don't know,' Enoch replied, 'But he seems to enjoy it. I watch him chuckling to himself sometimes.'

'Do you think he's going daft?' Brian asked in a hushed tone.

'Maybe,' Enoch answered, 'You never can tell.'

'Too true,' Alan supported.

'My dad says he's writing his life story,' Barry informed the gang.

'Wow!' Enoch exclaimed. 'That will take him all his life.'

'Obviously,' Rosie sneered.

'He will never get it finished,' Brian said mysteriously.

'Why?' Enoch wanted to know.

'Well. It stands to reason,' Brian explained, 'You can't write about your life, can you? Not all your life.'

'Why not?' Enoch pressed.

'Because,' Brian said heavily, 'How can you write about your last day on this earth, if you're dead the next day?'

'Oh, I see what you mean,' Enoch breathed. 'Yes. It's impossible isn't it? No-one can write their life story. Do you know, Brian, that is very good thinking on your part.'

'Thanks, Enoch,' Brian replied.

'I wonder where he'll start?' Margaret asked quietly.

'I suppose, at the day he was born,' Barry commented.

'Huh. That will be boring,' Enoch sneered, 'I can't see anybody wanting to read about that. I mean. The First Day. Got born this morning. Had a look around. Had a drink of milk. Had a sleep. Woke up. Had a cry. Had a sleep. Had a drink of milk. Boring. The Second Day. Woke up. Got tickled on the face by a grinning man. Had some boring milk. Had another boring sleep. Woke up. Bored as usual. Who'd want to read years of that stuff?'

'He could miss all that out,' Rosie defended, 'He could just write about the hinteresting time when he lost his leg. I bet that wasn't boring. I bet that was the most hinteresting time of his life. Losing a leg. Just fancy, one minute stood up OK. The next . . . toppling to one side, wondering where his other leg had buggered off to.'

The gang lapsed into silence and stared into their camp-fire in the hollow of their den on the bombed-site. Sometime later Enoch lolled back on his multi-purpose cushion which now acted as a back rest and said, 'Do you know, one day I think I'll ask Mr. Dent how he lost his leg. I mean, it's not very often you meet people who are careless enough to lose a leg, is it? I bet he has a very interesting story to tell about it.'

Alan nodded in agreement.

'Perhaps he wasn't careless,' Rosie commented, 'Perhaps he's absent-minded like professors and other brain-boxes. They're always losing and forgetting things, aren't they? No doubt being a nauthor makes him absent-minded and things. Perhaps he didn't lose his leg. Perhaps it just dropped off and he was too absent-minded to notice it at the time, and when he found out it was missing, perhaps he'd hopped away from wherever he'd lost it and couldn't remember where he'd been stood in the first place when he had both legs on.'

'What?' Enoch said incredulously, 'I've never heard so much daft talk since, er, since er . . . '

'See?' Margaret said with a smirk. 'Enoch's becoming absent-minded now. I'd be careful and keep a watch on your legs if I was you.'

Enoch tightened his lips into a thin line and scowled at laughing Margaret. 'Right. That does it,' he exploded, 'I'll show you lot. I'm off.'

'Where are you going?' Brian asked.

'I am going,' Enoch emphasised, 'to see Mr. Dent and ask him about his missing leg and his writing and things. I'll show you lot who's absent-minded.'

'Can you remember the way to his house?' Margaret sniggered.

Enoch's face contorted. His hands clenched until his knuckles grew white, then turning, he clambered from the hollow and marched determinedly across the ruins towards the distant houses, with a firm resolve to discover once and for all just what Mr. Dent had done with his missing leg.

*   *   *   *

'Hello, Mr. Dent,' Enoch said cheerfully as he sat on the high wall looking down into the small garden at the rear of the house. Mr. Dent looked up from his large note book, removed his elastoplastered glasses, squinted against the sunlight, shaded his eyes, focused them with some difficulty and, letting a smile stretch his full lips, answered, 'Why, hello. It's young Enoch isn't it?'

'Yes, It's me alright, Mr. Dent.'

'Well now, son, what can I do for you?'

'Mr. Dent,' Enoch replied, 'How did you lose your leg?'

'That's a funny question to be asking,' Mr. Dent said. 'Why do you ask?'

'Er, er, Margaret says you lost it because your mind is absent sometimes,' Enoch answered.

Mr. Dent smiled wryly. 'Did she now?' The old man chuckled.

Enoch nodded his head vigorously.

'Do you think that is true?'

'I don't know,' Enoch said. 'Is it?'

'Tell you what, son, why don't you climb down. I've just made a cup of tea. Would you like some?'

'No thanks,' Enoch replied, 'But I will come down, thank you.' He slipped from his perch and landed in the garden, then crossed to where the old man was sitting.

'Well now, Enoch. It's not very often I have company. This is an honour. Pull up that there box and sit down.'

Enoch did as he was told and sat expectantly, looking at Mr. Dent as he straightened his papers.

'Is that your fainemous life story, Mr. Dent?'

The writer smiled again and nodded.

'How far have you got?' Enoch questioned.

The old man's eyes twinkled. 'Oh, it's funny you should ask that, son. I've just finished writing about the time I lost my leg.'

Enoch became very interested and cupped his chin into his palms, 'How?' he breathed.

'Well, Enoch, I could say I lost it in the war, couldn't I? Or I could say that I lost it in an heroic accident. But no.' He bent towards Enoch and in a confidential tone said, 'I lost it in a far more exciting and interesting way.'

'How?' Enoch asked, wide-eyed.

Mr. Dent drew back, eyed Enoch, looked around as though frightened of being overheard, then said in a hushed voice, 'Polar Bears.'

Enoch's mouth dropped open and he breathed, 'Wow!'

Mr. Dent nodded solemnly.

'Wow! Polar Bears. How?'

Mr. Dent lifted his head and gazed at the white-washed wall with a faraway look in his eyes.

'It was like this, young Enoch. There we were, sailing our galleon . . . '

'Wow! A galleon.'

'Yes. A four-masted galleon. So, there we were, sailing it across the North Pole . . . '

'Wow! The North Pole.'

Mr. Dent nodded and pursed his lips, 'When all of a sudden my first mate shouts, "Captain!" That was me, you see,' he added as an aside. Enoch nodded his head vigorously.

'"Captain!" he shouts. "The ship is doomed. What shall your loyal and trusted crew do?" Quick as a flash I tells them to stop panicking – after all, panicking is no good, is it?'

Enoch shook his mesmerised head violently.

Mr. Dent continued, 'Panicking is no good at all. So I shouts, "Abandon ship".'

'Wow!'

'We packed all our belongings, and climbing down the side, we landed on the ice. Then we watched our ship, the good ship, er, oh I've forgot her name . . . '

'Probably that's his absent-mindedness doing that,' Enoch thought.

' . . . sink without a trace.'

'What happened next?'

'Well, there we were. All alone. Up at the North Pole. Floating about on a big lump of cold ice.'

Enoch shivered involuntarily.

'What were we to do?'

Enoch shook his head and breathed, 'I don't know.'

'I'll tell you what we did.'

'What?' Enoch whispered.

'We built an igloo and slept in it all safe and snug like. Me being captain, I decides to act as a look-out in case a ship passed in the night.'

'Very sensible,' Enoch thought, then added, 'And brave.'

'Well, during the night, that's when it happened.'

'What happened?' Enoch asked urgently.

'I heard this growl and then a roar. I looked around and saw this giant Polar Bear knocking our igloo down.'

'Blimey. What did you do?'

'Without thinking of my own safety . . . well you don't at times like that do you?' he asked.

Enoch shook his head firmly.

'I charged the Polar bear, and using my bare hands . . . these very ones,' he held them out for Enoch to look at, 'I began wrestling with it on the slippery ice.'

Enoch squirmed in excitement.

'On and on we fought. First he was winning, then I was winning. On and on. Then suddenly he did something which was very unfair.'

'What?' Enoch asked.

'He turned quickly, and before I could stop him, he bit my leg off, and running away, dived into the sea with it.'

'Flippin' 'eck!' Enoch exclaimed, 'That was a dirty trick.'

'Yes it was,' Mr. Dent said. 'I had all my family's jewels in that trouser pocket as well.' Then he added mysteriously, 'Mind you, he didn't get away with that dirty trick. I paid him back alright.'

'It's still shocking though,' Enoch breathed.

'Shocking indeed, young Enoch,' Mr. Dent agreed, turning his head away to hide a smile.

'Flippin' 'eck!' Enoch exclaimed. 'What an exciting thing to happen.'

Mr. Dent nodded his head, and then reaching out, tousled Enoch's hair.

'How did you get back home Mr. Dent?' Enoch asked.

'Now let me see,' the writer scratched his chin. 'Oh yes. Now I remember.'

'How?' Enoch said.

'Well, the following day a big whaling ship hoved into view and . . . '

'What's hoved?' Enoch questioned.

'Er. Appeared, like,' Mr. Dent answered.

'Oh. Hoved,' Enoch repeated, then added it to his collection of unusual and interesting words to impress the gang with.

'Yes. There it was parked right by our piece of ice. The Captain, now he was a Chinaman . . . '

'Wow! A Chinaman.'

'Yes,' Mr. Dent went on, 'A Chinaman. All the way from China. He hauled us all aboard and after many, many adventures hunting big white whales and other sea monsters, he dropped us off in the safety of our own country.'

'That was good of him,' Enoch said, rather matter of factly.

'Yes, it was wasn't it?' Mr. Dent bit his bottom lip to suppress his smile. 'And that, young Enoch, is how I lost my leg. But don't tell anyone, will you? I likes to keep it a secret. I'm not one for bragging you know.'

Enoch looked at him and shook his head solemnly. 'I understand, Mr. Dent. I don't like braggers either. I won't tell anyone.'

Mr. Dent flicked his head to one side, winked at Enoch, and said, 'Good lad.'

*   *   *   *

It was some weeks later that the gang heard the sad news that Mr. Dent had died. Enoch was very upset. After all, having found a new friend, and sharing that new friend's great secret, only to have him snatched away, seemed very unfair in his scheme of things. However, Mr. Dent did eventually slip from his ever-questioning mind, and he resumed his pre-occupation with the games of the gang. Occasionally his thoughts flitted to the writer. Just one thing puzzled Enoch. What had Mr. Dent done to pay the polar bear back for pinching his leg?

'Ah, well. I don't suppose I will ever know now,' he thought. But Enoch did get to know. And in a very surprising manner.

*   *   *   *

It was whilst the gang were playing hide and seek one day that Enoch found himself climbing the familiar wall and dropping into the deserted garden. It was quiet and still. The blank windows of the empty house seemed to watch him as he crossed the long grass, passed the neglected table, and approached a chaotic pile of hastily thrown-out furniture and the unwanted belongings of his friend. He stood in front of an old wardrobe and looked at his reflection in the yellowing, oxidised mirror. He reached and pushed the door shut, then half turning to look at a jumble of old, damp, mildewed clothes, he shivered and suddenly felt a little frightened. There was a moaning creak and a knock on his shoulder. He jumped and spun his head, then sighed through blown out cheeks. The wardrobe door had swung open again. Taking a nervous step to one side, he peered around the back of precariously piled furniture. Suddenly he heard Rosie's voice call out, 'Coming. Ready or not.'

The game. He'd forgotten the game. With a quick movement he flung himself behind the wardrobe to hide. His foot caught a cardboard box. There was a thud. The pile of furniture moved, and before Enoch knew what was happening, he found himself buried under the discarded, musty belongings. Recovering, he saw daylight through a gap between the cooker and the settee and pushed his way towards it. Opening the gap and pushing his head through, he froze in horror. Only inches from his face was the great wide, snarling mouth of a Polar Bear. Enoch yelled, panicked then fell into the freedom of the deathly quiet yard. Scrambling to his feet he half turned and looked over his shoulder.

'Flippin' 'eck,' he hissed as his eyes fell on the Polar Bear's head once more. 'Blimey. It's stuffed.'

He stood staring at the enormous grinning head for some moments. Mr. Dent's story came flooding back in all its detail.

'So that was it. That's how Mr. Dent got his own back. The Bear pinched his leg, and so Mr. Dent pinched the Polar Bear's head,' Enoch reasoned. 'That's a fair swop.'

He approached it and bending down, tentatively touched the fur. It was cold and stiff. Enoch's eyes were suddenly caught by a pile of note books and bundles of neatly written papers.

'Wow! Mr. Dent's life story,' he breathed. 'Chucked out and unwanted. It's disgustable.'

He reached and began stacking the books into a neat pile at the side of the mounted head.

'Poor old Mr. Dent,' he thought, 'Gone and forgotten by his near-nest and dear-nest. Shocking. Well, I'll not forget you Captain Dent. I'll save your books and when I learn to read better, I'll tell everybody what a great heroic hero you was. And I'll keep your Polar Bear's head as proof of your exciting adventures. Don't you worry, Captain Dent. I'll see to it that no-one ever forgets you.'

Enoch reached and lifted the heavy head up by the upper jaw and the back of the wooden plaque. As he did so he felt something soft and thin inside the grinning mouth. His hand moved and an old shoe lace dropped to the ground.

'Wow!' he exclaimed, 'That proves it. Mr. Dent's long-forgotten North Pole shoe lace from his lost leg. And still in the Polar Bear's mouth. What a souvenir.'

Hair-raising Gossip

****

MRS. FRANCES JACKMAN was the area's chronicler of all things vaguely scandalous. Her mind was a vast repository of neighbourhood arguments, scandalous goings on, and anything that didn't fit into her moral code of behaviour. A code which she was at pains to explain to anyone careless enough to venture a 'Good morning' at her. When gossip was in the offing, her enormous, round body could be seen scuttling from one lace-curtained, terraced house to the next, gathering a tit-bit here and leaving a germ of disquiet there.

If gossip plus a scandal reared into view she positively floated along, giving the illusion of being blown by the wind. But if one looked closely, her tiny carpetslippered feet could be seen working away like pistons, carrying her wobbling bulk ever onward, to dispense half-truths, knowing nods of head, and countless 'tuts' and 'disgustings.' Housework to Mrs. Frances Jackman was an intrusion into her career of character assassination and so housework was never attempted. She left those mundane tasks to her nonentity of a husband, who was owner of the local barber shop, and who had long since built a brick wall around himself, climbed in, and preferred to get life over with, instead of living it. Mrs. Francis Jackman was not a nice person.

'World War Three must have broken out,' Alan remarked. 'Just look at her go.'

The gang looked up and saw Mrs. Jackman attaining supersonic speed as she raced along the pavement with her arms folded under her enormous, pinafored breasts.

'It must be good gossip,' Rosie said. 'I've not seen her move so fast since Mrs. Ryan was dying and she'd been promised her three pot ducks.'

'My Mam sez she wears out six pairs of slippers a year,' Margaret announced. 'At that speed it's a wonder we can't see smoke coming from them.'

The gang continued to watch as Mrs. Jackman turned down the first terraced-house entry on her never-ending round of dishing out great dollops of hearsay to her favoured band of selected listeners.

'She'd be quicker if she bought herself a bicycle,' Herbert said, as he continued prising mortar from around a brick which was set in the boundary wall of the vicarage.

'They don't make saddles that big,' Enoch sniffed.

The gang giggled.

Mrs. Jackman re-appeared at the top of the entry, looked up and down the street, sniffed the air, then shot off towards her next appointment with malice. Her cheeks were flushed with the glow of gossip. She was followed closely by Mrs. Lindley, who, wearing the official badge of gossiper second class, namely arms folded under slightly smaller breasts, galloped off in the opposite direction to spread the bulletin, plus embellishments, to her own group of disseminators of all things shocking and sniggery.

Soon the street was busy with pinafored carriers of tidings criss-crossing the road, in and out of houses, and generally having a high old time of it, until the story lost all semblance of its original content, retaining only the names of the main actors.

Eventually the street emptied and they all returned to their firesides to await further scandal, whereupon the whole fascinating process would start again, ceasing only when husbands returned from work for their evening meal.

Herbert had lost interest in constructing a secret safe in the vicarage wall, the mortar proving too stubborn, and now turned his attention to collecting spider's webs from the dusty privet hedge, using a tiny forked stick.

Margaret, with the help of Rosie, was endeavouring to do the splits. Her knickers were having more success than she, and a tearing sound issued from her rear. Enoch, Brian and Alan had removed the laces from their boots and, fashioning a noose, were about to dispatch Rosie's doll to the hereafter for crimes against anything which entered their heads. Barry sat to one side on the pavement edge, and carried out his role of a famous explorer. He was endeavouring to find the lost route to his brain via his left nostril. A boulder blocked the path. It was his eye ball.

*　*　*　*

'That's unusual,' Rosie remarked, as she watched Mr. Brigham returning home. 'That's the fourth time this week he's pushed his bike home.'

'Yes,' Enoch answered, 'He's got a puncture.'

'Well, why does he take the bike to work with him every day?' Rosie queried.

'He says the exercise does him good,' Enoch replied blandly.

'Oh,' Rosie replied, then returned to her task of supporting Margaret who was now attempting handstands.

'Doesn't the world look funny when you're upside down?' Margaret said through a mass of hair.

'Not half as funny as your torn knickers look,' Alan chuckled.

Margaret lost her balance and toppled to one side. She sat glaring at Alan. There was a muffled yell as Barry found a particularly sensitive nerve inside his head. His finger hurriedly returned to base camp and he wiped tears from his eyes. Brian was endeavouring to keep the doll's eyes shut, feeling it was aesthetically more pleasing to have a freshly-hanged doll with eyes closed rather than open. He solved the problem by wedging two dirty spent match sticks under the lids, then stood back to admire the result of his ingenuity.

'So die all bad people,' he mumbled to himself, then lost interest as he saw Herbert peering under his arm.

'What're you looking at?' he asked.

Herbert glanced up and across at Brian. 'I've got a hair,' he breathed.

'What?' Brian questioned.

'I've got a hair under my arm. Look!'

Brian bent to examine Herbert's armpit.

'That means you're growing up.'

'What does?' Rosie called.

'Herbert's got a hair under his arm,' Brian informed her. 'He's going to grow up soon.'

'I don't believe you,' Rosie answered.

'He has!' Brian exclaimed. 'Come and look.'

Rosie and Margaret crossed to Herbert, and stooping, peered at the arm-pit.

'That's a grown-up hair is that,' Herbert said proudly. 'It's the first one I've had.'

Margaret reached and made to touch it.

'Don't pull it out,' Herbert glared indignantly. 'It's taken me a long time to grow that.'

'I wasn't going to pull it out. I was only going to feel it.'

'Well you can't,' Herbert said firmly.

'Just a minute!' Rosie exclaimed. 'It's blue.'

'What is?' Brian asked.

'His hair. It's blue.'

They all peered closely.

'So it is,' Margaret said.

'That's not a hair,' Rosie sneered. 'It's a piece of blue cotton. Look.' She quickly snatched and pulled at the thread.

'See,' she said triumphantly. 'Look!' Rosie held the cotton for all to see. 'It's only cotton.'

They began to laugh.

'Well it could have been a hair,' Herbert defended, and then began to sulk as he realised manhood had eluded him yet again.

'When I grow up,' he mumbled, 'I'm going to grow as many hairs as I like. I'll be the hairiest grown-up around here. You watch. You'll not laugh then.'

'Me mam sez that Mr. Chippinghouse is going bald,' Barry announced.

'Mr. Chippinghouse says he's not bothered. He says grass doesn't grow on a busy street.'

'What's grass growing in the street got to do with going bald?' Enoch asked.

'Well, you know,' Barry answered, 'Grass doesn't grow on a busy street because . . . er . . . people are always walking on it and . . . er . . . kicking it out by its roots.'

'Well, I still don't see what growing grass has got to do with going bald,' Enoch said. 'I mean, I shouldn't think many people from around here walk across Mr. Chippinghouse's head very often. In fact, I bet no-one 'as ever walked over his head. Unless he was lying down or something.'

'That's true,' Brian supported. Barry decided not to pursue the topic. He wasn't quite sure of the relationship of grass, hair, and Mr. Chippinghouse's head.

'I wish I was bald,' Alan announced.

'Why?' Rosie questioned.

'Well, I wouldn't have to have my hair washed and combed. I hate that. And I wouldn't have to go to Mr. Jackman's for cutting it. He's got blunt scissors and he doesn't half pull at your roots.'

'And the dicks and nits wouldn't have a home would they?' Enoch added. 'No more nit-comb to worry about. It would be great.'

'Yes. Just a quick wipe with the flannel and it would be washed,' Barry supported.

'I mean,' Enoch continued, 'What use is hair on your head anyway? It always needs cutting and washing and combing and things. Hair is a complete waste of human energy. Isn't it?'

'Hair gives you strength,' Rosie said knowingly. 'If you cut it all off you'd be dead weak. Samson found that out when that dead woman gave him a haircut years ago in the desert of a foreign country.'

'Well, it's not surprising that Sam's son got weak is it?' Enoch said scornfully. 'His dad should know better than to send Sam to a woman barber. Haircutting is a man's job. Not a woman's. I bet, really, that Sam's dad sent him to the barbers, but the barber was out or something. I bet it was his wife who cut Sammy's hair so she could get some extra housekeeping money without her husband knowing. I bet his dad went mad when he saw Sam crawling home all weak and wiv hardly any hair on his nut. I bet he got his money back alright.'

'It's a good job Mr. Jackman doesn't let his wife near his scissors, isn't it?' Herbert said.

'Fancy having your hair cut by Fanny Jackman!' Barry exclaimed. 'Ugh. That would be horrible.'

'Yes. She'd natter you to death, wouldn't she?' Brian said.

'See? See? See what I mean?' Enoch said eagerly. 'It's bad enough having to have your hair cut at all, but having to listen to Fanny Jackman as well, wow, that would mek anyone weak at these knees of ours.'

'Yes. At least Mr. Jackman is quiet, isn't he?' Barry said.

The gang all nodded in agreement then fell silent as Mrs. Frances Jackman appeared once more, scuttling along with fresh gossip.

They sat on the pavement edge and watched her disappear down Mrs. Brigham's entry.

'She saves all the hair that Mr. Jackman cuts off.' Margaret said quietly.

'What for?' Enoch asked.

'My mam sez she bags it up and sells it to foreign countries.'

'What for?' Alan queried.

'They stuff things with it.'

'Well, of all the flippin' cheek!' Enoch exploded. 'We spend all our time growing it. Then Mr. Jackman cuts it off and charges us. Then she collects it and sells it to foreigners. Flippin' 'eck.'

'Mr. Chippinghouse knows what he's doing, doesn't he? No wonder he's decided to go bald. He'll save himself a fortune, won't he? I bet that's what he means about grass not growing on a busy street. Particularly this one. Fanny Jackman is wearing it out with her hair-raising tales and gossiping feet.'

The gang agreed.

Invisible Earnings

'**A**ND NOW, ladies and genklemen, here at last, for you all to look at, Enoch, the Invisible Man.' Brian's announcement was to the sea of unwashed, jam-coated, miniature faces that stared with unblinking eyes at the piece of torn curtain which hung between Alan's outside toilet wall and the clothes post which lolled in the unkempt grass of his small back garden.

The curtain twitched then suddenly parted, and Enoch stood before the crowd, wearing on his head a brown paper bag with two eye slits in it. From the long sleeves of an old jacket his concealed hands held his mother's two rubber gloves which were stuffed with cotton wool. Wrapped around his legs were sheets of newspaper.

'He's not invisible. I can see him,' a voice jeered from somewhere to the rear of the motley audience.

'Hah-ah!' Brian exclaimed, 'that's the clever part. You think you can see the invisible Enoch, but no, it's only his clothes and visibility paper you can see. No, ladies and genklemen, underneath his visibility dress he is completely invisible. Aren't you, oh mighty Enoch?'

Enoch nodded. The brown paper bag rustled.

'And now, ladies and genklemen, Enoch-the-unseeable will perform some invisible tricks. Watch carefully, everybody. The juggling with ten invisible plates trick,' Brian bawled.

Enoch raised the dummy hands and began waggling them up and down. A mumbling came from the restless audience but it was effectively silenced when Alan, who was concealed behind the curtain, threw an old plate to the ground and Enoch made a great show of picking up the invisible pieces.

'Even the best invisible jugglers make mistakes, ladies and genklemen,' Brian called. Then inspiration struck and he added hastily, 'We will be selling souvenir pieces of the broken invisible plate after the show. They will be a penny a piece. This will enable you to show your forefathers in your after-life, which you are all going to grow up into, that you saw Enoch-the-invisible perform.'

'That was a very clever trick,' called Barry, who had planted himself in the audience earlier. 'Well done, oh Enoch-the-invincible.'

'Invisible,' Brian corrected.

'Yer. Him as well,' Barry shouted back and began clapping as arranged earlier. The audience, like sheep, followed suit.

'And now, ladies and genklemen, the moment you have had to wait for. Enoch-the-invisible will prove to you all and sundry that he is really invisible.'

The audience became more attentive as they watched Enoch stumble his way around the back of the curtain. There was a pause, and then, first one rubber glove was thrown over the top of the curtain, and then the other. Enoch reappeared and waved the sleeves of the jacket about. 'Look everybody,' Brian called, 'Now you can't see his hands.'

There were 'Wows,' and gasps, mainly from Barry, as Enoch pranced around.

'Ladies and genklemen, Enoch-the-not-seen would take more of his clothes off but it is very cold and he doesn't want to catch his deathness.'

'How about his paper head, then?' a voice called.

'Ladies and genklemen. Enoch has a very bad case of ear-ache and has to keep it warm. That is why he's keeping his bag on. So, ladies and genklemen the show is over for today. Thank you for coming and don't forget to buy some invisible plate on your way out. Thank you.'

Brian and Enoch quickly vacated the make-shift stage, and together with Alan of the props department they climbed the garden wall and headed for the safety of their secret emergency den behind the neighbourhood vicarage, with new money chinking in their pockets.

'How much did we make?' Barry asked, as he joined the gang sometime later.

'Eightpence each,' Enoch informed him.

'Wow. That's smashing,' Barry breathed.

'How many pieces of invisible plate did you sell?' Brian asked.

'None,' Barry replied. 'I couldn't find where you'd put the invisible pieces.'

Alan rolled his eyes and sighing said, 'You burke! That was the whole point. All you had to do was to pretend to wrap pieces up and sell them.'

'Oh,' Barry said feeling rather dejected, 'Sorry.'

'It doesn't matter,' Enoch said. 'Eightpence each isn't bad, is it? Almost a shilling. Cheer up, Barry. Here's your money. We understand.'

'Thanks, Enoch. Thanks,' Barry gushed. 'I'll go back later and have a good look for that invisible plate. Sorry I didn't manage to find it. But it's there somewhere, I know it is.'

Brian, Alan, and Enoch looked at each other with resigned expressions on their faces, then shrugging their shoulders, they smiled kindly at Barry.

*   *   *   *

'Hello, you lot,' Rosie said brightly as she jumped down into the hollow. 'I thought I'd find you here. Mr. Topham's looking for you, Enoch.'

'What for?' Enoch asked on the defensive.

'Don't know. But he keeps muttering about disappearing tricks and skinning you alive when he finds you, and something about taking money from his Arnold.'

'Fraid I can't help him there,' Enoch said. 'I'm totally innocence about his Arnold's penny, aren't we?' he turned to the rest of the gang for confirmation.

'Yer,' they answered.

'Why are your legs parceled up in newspaper?' Rosie asked.

'It's a secret,' Enoch answered. 'Now stop asking nosey questions. And stop shouting. This is a secret den, you know. Not public property.'

Rosie sat in the crushed grass and, pulling her cotton bobbin from her dress pocket, began nail-knitting. 'You lot have been up to something, haven't you?' she said quietly without taking her eyes from her busy hair grip.

'No, we haven't,' Alan said in all innocence. 'We've been sat here all morning. Haven't we Brian?'

'Too true, Alan,' Brian supported. 'I was just saying to Enoch here, "Do you know, Enoch, we've been sat in this den all day, haven't we?"'

Rosie raised her head and gave him her special, 'I don't believe a word you're saying,' look.

'Mind you,' Enoch said meaningfully, 'I was just answering Brian by saying, "I think I'll spend the rest of the day here amongst this peaceful grass." It's very nice here.'

Rosie transferred her look to him and said, 'Are you sure it's got nothing to do with mad Mr. Topham?'

'Certainly not,' Enoch shot back.

'Well, if you lot are going to stop here all day,' Barry announced suddenly, 'I think I'll go back to the stage and hunt for that invisible plate.'

Enoch, Alan, and Brian groaned.

'Hah,' Rosie said in triumph, 'I knew you'd been up to something. What invisible plate, Barry?'

'Enoch can make himself invisible,' Barry said proudly. 'He did it this morning at a show we put on for the neighbourhood children. It only cost them a penny each to look at him. Didn't it Enoch?'

'You burke,' Enoch exploded.

'I only charge fourpence to keep a secret,' Rosie said matter-of-factly. The gang didn't argue. Arguing, they knew, was pointless when Rosie held the whip hand. Reluctantly the three reached into their pockets and, being careful not to jangle the remaining money, in case she suddenly had an attack of avarice, they removed a penny apiece and handed it to a beaming Rosie.

'You can keep your penny, Barry, for being honest with me,' she said generously, as she slipped the coins inside her knicker leg.

'Hello, everybody,' Margaret called as she pushed her way into the clearing through the thick bushes. 'Mr. Topham is looking for you, Enoch.'

'Oh shut up,' Enoch snarled, 'I'm fed up of hearing about Mr. Topham. You'd think he'd find something better to do than hunt and prostitute me every five minutes of my lifeness.'

'What have you been up to?' Margaret persisted.

'Nothing,' Enoch said forcefully.

Rosie sat with her head bent over her cotton bobbin wearing a smug smile. 'He's been taking money from Mr. Topham's Arnold.'

'Ah. That's stealing,' Margaret said righteously.

'Look, you two,' Enoch menaced, 'I didn't steal any money. He paid to see the invisible man, and that's what he saw.'

'How can you see an invisible man?' Margaret pursued the topic.

'You're looking at one,' Rosie chuckled.

'Why are your legs bundled up?' Margaret asked. 'Are they poorly?'

'No,' Enoch said miserably. 'They were part of my act.'

'What act?'

'Forget it. Alright?' Enoch requested with a hint of menace in his voice.

'There is no such thing as invisible things,' Margaret carried on. 'Either you can see something or it doesn't exist.'

'What about air?' Brian said.

'What about it?'

'Well, you can't see air, can you?'

'No.'

'Well, there you are then. You can't see air but you can feel it and smell it, can't you?' Brian said confidently.

'And invisible ink,' Alan joined in. 'That's dead handy stuff for spies, isn't it?'

'Suppose so,' Margaret agreed, losing the argument.

'Oh yes. There's tons of other invisible things alright,' Barry said. 'In fact, I'm just off to try and find an invisible plate, aren't I Enoch?'

Enoch closed his eyes and shook his head with a resigned expression on his face.

'I wonder if you drank invisible ink you'd become invisible?' Brian pondered.

'Light is invisible,' Alan suddenly said.

'Don't talk daft,' Rosie sneered. 'Everyone can see light. If we couldn't, it would be dark all the time. Every day would be full of night time.'

Alan ignored her. 'Light is invisible,' he emphasised. 'It's what it settles on that we see. But we never, ever, see light. Not in all our lifeness. Light is definitely invisible.'

'Look,' Enoch exploded, 'Once and for all. Stop talking about invisibleness. Alright? Talk about something else for a change.'

The gang fell silent, realising Enoch's temper was at breaking point.

'Well, I'll be off.' Barry rose to his feet.

'Where are you going?' Rosie baited.

'I'm going to look for that invisi . . . er, er. Oh, just for a walk,' Barry corrected and glanced at tight-lipped Enoch who was unwrapping his legs. He pushed through the bushes and they heard his whistling fade into the distance.

'Mrs. Brigham's cat mauled Mrs. Cookson's budgie last week,' Margaret informed the gang. 'She only left its little door open for a few minutes – to give it a breath of fresh air, I think – and whoosh, Sheba was in there causing chaos. Mr. Cookson is making it a little wooden leg from a matchstick.'

'Ah. Poor old Chuckle Bun,' Rosie sympathised.

'Chuckle Bun!' Enoch exclaimed in disbelief. 'Chuckle Bun? That's a daft name for a budgie. Fancy calling a budgie Chuckle Bun!'

'I think it's a nice name,' Rosie defended.

'You would,' Enoch retorted.

'It's not whistled or banged its bell once since that fateful day,' Margaret went on. 'Mrs. Cookson says all it does is balance on its one good leg on the perch and keep looking nervously over its little shoulder.'

Suddenly Brian collapsed back into the grass, howling with laughter.

'What's so funny?' Margaret asked.

'I've just thought of a joke,' Brian choked.

'What?' Enoch asked. 'Come on, tell us.'

'Who covers himself in bread and potted meat, puts a tomato in each ear, and swings on a bell?' Brian asked amid renewed laughter.

'Don't know,' Alan answered.

'The lunch pack of Notre Dame!' Brian roared.

The corners of Enoch's mouth twitched and he found himself laughing along with the rest of them, until the bushes echoed with their happiness.

'So this is where you're hiding,' a deep voice bellowed from above them. The gang froze and stared up into the stern face of Mr. Topham, who stood with his hands on his hips.

'Now then you lot, who's got our Arnold's penny?'

'We don't know what you mean, Mr. Topham,' Enoch feigned innocence.

'Don't give me that. You took a penny from our Arnold this morning to see a daft show. Now come on, own up, you little varmints.'

'Oow. We're not little varmints,' Rosie protested. 'That's a wicked thing to call innocent children. We wouldn't dream of pinching money from your Arnold. We've been brought up to be honest and truthful in everything we do. And now you're saying we pinched money. It's not fair,' Rosie said and then pretended to cry.

Enoch quickly took the cue and added, 'Don't cry, Rosie. We're used to being blamed for everything that goes wrong. Be brave.'

'Well, look, er,' Mr. Topham said awkwardly, 'I didn't mean you'd stolen his penny. I, er, er, meant you took it off him.'

'No we didn't,' Alan joined in. 'Your Arnold gave it to us. Why. he practically forced it on us. We didn't want to take it because we knew he'd be in trouble from you, Mr. Topham, when you found out. I said at the time. I said, 'Look, Arnold, keep your penny. We don't want your penny. We wouldn't dream of asking you for your penny.' But your Arnold practically pushed it at us. Didn't he?' Alan asked.

'Yes,' Rosie sobbed.

'That's true,' Enoch supported.

'Oh,' Mr. Topham said with an unsure note in his voice. 'I didn't realise.'

'Oh yes,' Brian took up the crusade, 'Oh yes, Mr. Topham. We like your Arnold very much. Very much indeed. But he is a bit daft with his money. He's always giving it away to people. We keep telling him don't we?' Brian turned and directed the question at his fellow accused. 'We say, "Arnold, keep your money safe in your pocket. Don't keep giving it away. Especially to us. We don't want it. We like you just as a friend."'

Mr. Topham was mellowing fast. Rosie continued to sob.

'Oh, I didn't realise,' he repeated. 'Sorry, kids. Sorry if I upset you.'

'That's alright,' Enoch said heavily. 'We're used to it.' Then added, 'If it wasn't for the friendship in our gang, and the supportness we give each other, even though we never have any money to spend on sweets, I don't know what we would do.'

'Look,' Mr. Topham said, who was now effectively puttied, 'Look kids. Here. Take this. Buy yourselves some spice.' He held out sixpence.

'We mustn't take money from strange men,' Rosie sobbed.

'Oh, I'm sure it will be alright this time.' Mr. Topham cajoled.

'Well, alright,' Enoch feigned reluctance whilst at the same time palming the money. 'Thank you, Mr. Topham.'

'Sorry I accused you,' Mr. Topham apologised, ruffling Enoch's hair in a friendly gesture. He turned and began pushing his way back into the bushes.

'Enoch. Enoch,' Barry's excited voice burst into the clearing from the opposite side of the hollow. 'Enoch. Enoch. Guess what? I've just seen daft Arnold Topham in the street. Guess what? I fooled him into buying the whole bagful of invisible plate. Look. Look. He gave me sixpence for an empty bag.'

A bellowing roar sounded and Mr. Topham reappeared. The gang's hearts yo-yoed between their Adams' apples and their wellington-booted feet. Enoch let out a groan and suddenly wished, dearly wished, that he had a gallon of invisible ink handy to swallow.

The Decline and Fall
of Negypt

* * * * * * * * * * * * * * * * * * * *

'CAN ANYBODY tell me the capital of Egypt?' Mr. Marshall stood before the disinterested class of miniature Britons. A gentle breeze wafted over him as thirty heads shook in unison.

'Does anybody know where Egypt is?'

The breeze answered him.

'Does anybody know anything?'

Heads faltered in their shaking, then gathered confidence, and shook with renewed vigour. Mr. Marshall closed his eyes, clenched his fists, and wondered why he had bothered to seek a career in the teaching and beating profession. So far the emphasis had been on the latter, and the former was in danger of never being used. Sometimes he lay awake worrying about his increasing preoccupation of finding new tortures to inflict on his captive pupils. His recurring nightmare was to one day enter his classroom and spend the entire day in an orgy of punishing young bodies. He shuddered, and opening his eyes, gazed once more at the sea of dusty heads which it was his responsibility to fill with knowledge. Yet, now, as he looked, something was different. A hand was in the air. His heart leapt with joy. 'Yes, Lorretta?' he asked eagerly.

'Please sir. Enoch Thompson keeps making funny noises with his bum.'

'Ooo, Sir. It's not me. It's Rosie Bacon.'

'You're a liar, Enoch Thompson. It came from your direction.'

'It's an echo,' Enoch defended. 'It came from over by the windows.'

All heads turned to where Alan sat smirking.

'I can't help it, Sir. I've had beans for me breakfast.'

'Alright. Alright everybody. Settle down. Alan. Try to control yourself.'

Alan wondered how that was going to be possible.

'Right, you lot, turn to page thirty-seven in your geography books.' Mr. Marshall stood patiently until the thunder of desk lids and the gale of rustling pages died down.

'Today I shall be teaching you about Egypt,' he said sternly, and launched into a general account of the Nile delta, travelling upstream, and back in time. To his amazement he had the class's attention as he lectured them about the ancient Pharaohs and pyramids. Enoch became engrossed, as did all the gang, and when the school bell sounded it was a reluctant class that returned to the present day, and an elated teacher who climbed into Miss Fillibut's car for his customary lift to the outer suburbs, and his clinically clean house and wife.

Rosie stood on the bombed-site with an old net curtain wrapped about her body and a short piece of black. ribbed, hose-pipe, poking from the top-side of her infamous navy blue knickers.

'I'm Cleopatra,' she intoned, desperately trying to inject a note of mystery and allure into her voice. 'I am the Queen of all the Nile . . . both upper and lower. Bring me my Pharaoh.'

Alan and Brian stepped forward and frog-marched Barry into the gang's favourite meeting place.

'Watch it,' Barry menaced. 'You're hurting my arms.'

'Silence,' Cleopatra commanded. 'Bring my Pharaoh here.'

The two eunuchs pushed Barry towards Rosie.

'What do you want?' Barry asked.

'You don't say that,' Rosie hissed. 'You say . . . What can I do for you, oh Queen of all the Negypt.'

'Oh sorry,' Barry apologised. 'What can I do for you.'

'Fetch me some sweet meats . . . I want to feed my asp . . . He's hungry,' Rosie said, stroking the rubber pipe.

'You want to be careful, oh my Queen . . . Them snakes aren't half dangerous in the wrong hands. If he stings you it will cause your deathness, oh Queen of Negypt.'

'It's OK, Barry,' Rosie whispered, 'He's a tame un . . . He's never bitten me . . . They don't bite Queens.'

Barry nodded knowingly.

'I shall be off now, my Queen, to fetch you some meat that's sweet from the egyptian butchers. I won't be long, so don't pine for me.'

'Go now, oh Pharaoh . . . I'll be waiting on my throne when you come back from the shops. Tell the butcher to put it on the royal slate until the weekend.'

'Right-o,' Barry answered and exited stage left, tripping over a piece of broken floorboard in the process.

'I must get a new palace built soon,' Rosie sighed. 'This place is falling to bits.'

Enoch stood some way away and lifting a broken drain pipe to his mouth, he blew a fanfare.

'Hark,' Rosie said, 'My trusted trodden on slaves are returning from the pyramids what they are building for me . . . I bet they are hungry. It's way past their tea-time.'

Enoch marched towards them slashing and lashing at imaginary slaves. 'Down, you dogs. March faster . . . Aaahh . . . Ooooow . . . Take that you landlubbers.' Eventually he entered the circle and bowed before Rosie.

'Ullo, slave driver,' Cleopatra greeted Enoch.

'Ullo, my Queen,' Enoch replied.

'Have yer had a hard day?'

'I've never stopped whipping and driving my slaves about since I got up this morning. Mind you, the pyramid is coming along alright. We've finished making the pointed top, now all we have to do is to build the rest of it.'

'Well done, my slave driver. I'll buy you a posh new whip as a thank-you when it's finished.'

'Will it be a long one with barbed wire at the end?' Egyptian Enoch asked eagerly.

Cleopatra nodded.

'Thank you, oh my Queen of all Negypt. It's great working for you on the building site.'

'You may go and have your Egyptian tea now. Mek sure you're not late for work in the morning or I'll have to half-hour you.'

'Right-o,' Enoch answered cheerfully and bowed from Cleopatra's presence.

Suddenly, Herbert the eunuch ran into the clearing. 'My Queen . . . My Queen. Terrible news.'

'Whatever's up,' Rosie asked, 'You look as though you've seen a Mummy.'

'Oh my Queen . . . My Queen of all the Negypt . . . Bad news. The Nile has flooded again and the fields along its banks are covered with Nile water. The crops could be ruined.'

Rosie held her hand to her brow in anguish. 'Oh, my poor slaves and prisoners. I hope none of them are drowned or even worse, dead. That's the hundredth time this year that the river has bust it's banks . . . we're going to have to do something about it or I'll have no Kingdom left.'

'Queendom,' Herbert hissed.

'Yes, that as well,' Rosie answered. 'I suppose we'll be eating damp dates for a fortnight again. Leave me in my torment. I must shed Egyptian Queen tears in my chamber pot. Oh, oh, oh.'

Herbert clambered back over the house-bricks whilst Rosie sank to the ground and wept and wailed.

Pharaoh Barry returned from the butchers. 'Eeeh, lass. Whatever's the matter. I said I wouldn't be long . . . don't take on so. Here's your sweet meat.' He handed

Rosie some screwed-up newspaper containing four stones.

'Thank you, my Pharaoh, you are good to me. Oh these are my favourites. No, no, I wasn't pining for you, it's the river, it's flooded the fields and the prisoners have perished.'

'Don't worry, oh my Queen. I'll go and buy you some more from another King tomorrow. Now get yer grub down you and don't forget to feed yer snake. I've noticed that he's getting very thin.'

Enoch whispered to Alan, 'If I had to spend half my life down Rosie's knickers, I'd be looking a bit thin by now, wouldn't you?'

Alan giggled and nodded. Rosie didn't hear the aside, which was just as well. Her indian burns were legendary.

Margaret crossed into the circle wearing her mother's fox-fur stole. As she approached Cleopatra the fox's head dragged in the dust, it's glass eyes staring vacantly into the evening sky.

'Aaah, my hand-maiden. Come to attend my every need and want,' Rosie breathed. 'Speak, oh hand-maiden. What you got to tell me?'

Margaret made to curtsy but stumbled on a broken brick. She lost her balance and sat heavily down on the fox's head. There was a cracking sound and a glass eye rolled from under her and lay in the dust. Margaret recovered herself and said, 'Oh, Queen Cleopatra of the Nile, bad news.'

'Not more bad news,' Rosie sighed.

'Fraid so,' Margaret said with relish.

'What's up now?' Cleopatra asked.

'It's the pyramid. It's fallen down.' Enoch stood shocked at the gall of Margaret for bringing into question his building capabilities.

'She's talking rubbish. Don't believe her . . . that's a good pyramid . . . it'll never fall down . . . It must be one of the others . . . not mine. She's just trying to cause trouble, that's all.'

'No I'm not. It has fallen down, I tell you. There are millions of slaves dead and four camels as well.'

'Oh. Oh. Oh. Not the camels,' Cleopatra wailed. 'I loved them camels. They were like my own children. What are we going to do now?'

'We could have camel sandwiches,' Barry whispered.

Rosie rounded on Barry. 'I heard that . . . It's not funny. Now shut yer gob or I'll shut it for you.'

'You and whose army?' Barry threatened.

'Me and myself.'

'I'd like to see you try.'

'Just you wait. I'll get you,' Rosie answered.

'Well, you'd better make sharp before all your Kingdom collapses into the river,' Barry laughed.

Rosie turned from him and climbed back into her role of Cleopatra. She wasn't going to let anybody spoil her death scene. She faltered for a few seconds then became once more the most famous Queen that ever lived.

'It is too much,' she cried. 'I'm fed up with all this responsibility. Never have I yearned for death so much. When I am gone don't you lot yearn for your dead Queen. Remember me as I am now. A young and beautiful Queen of Negypt. It's no use yearning over spilled milk when I'm gone . . . yearning never solved anything.'

Yearning was Rosie's latest favourite word. She was flogging it to death. 'Yearn not, my people. Bury me in my pyramid when I am dead.'

'We can't,' Pharaoh Barry said. 'It's fallen down.'

'Well, build me another,' Rosie glared and snapped back at him. She turned to the rest of the gang. 'I shall kill myself in a minute, my people. Remember what a good Queen I was and tell all your friends to put flowers on my new pyramid every year and to keep it free of weeds.' Rosie slowly pulled the length of hosepipe from her knickers and wiggled it about in front of her chest.

'It's a lively bugger isn't it?' Enoch whispered.

Brian nodded. 'I expect it's glad to get some fresh air.'

Suddenly and quite unexpectedly Rosie pressed the end of the pipe to her chest and let out a blood-curdling scream. All the gang jumped and watched as she rolled her eyes into her head and made a guttural sound in her throat. Margaret was quite caught up in the story and whimpered as Rosie fell to her knees. 'Aaaah the pain,' she uttered, 'I'm going. The lights grow dim. Farewell all of my subjects. I'll be dead shortly,' Rosie slumped into the dust.

'We'd better get on wiv burying her – you know how bodies go off quickly in hot countries,' Enoch said.

Rosie lifted her head from the ground. 'I'm not dead yet. Don't you be so anxious, Enoch Thompson.'

Enoch stepped back a pace. 'Well hurry up Rosie . . . I mean, Queen Cleopatra. We can't wait all day.'

'Oh, Oh the pain!' Rosie shouted. Margaret jumped.

'I'll be giving my death rattle in a minute. Listen for it . . . I do it good.' The Queen's subjects drew nearer and formed a circle around their expiring Queen. A long, drawn-out, strangled sound issued from her.

'She's rattling,' Margaret whispered. They all stood staring down at the still form of the Queen of Negypt.

'Rosie. Rosie. Are you dead?' Herbert said in a hushed tone.

Rosie nodded her head.

'Right,' Enoch said in a business like manner, 'Let's bury her.'

The two eunuchs stepped forward and lifted their Queen to her feet. The gang formed a small procession and slowly, supporting a half-stumbling, half-walking Rosie, made their way towards the site of Enoch's pyramid. Reaching the site they put Rosie on the ground.

'It's a smashing pyramid!' Barry exclaimed. 'Did you build it all by yourself, Enoch?'

Enoch swelled with pride as he answered, 'Yes.'

'It's just like that picture in Mr. Marshall's book,' Brian complimented Enoch.

'It must have taken you hours to build it, Enoch,' Margaret fawned.

Enoch smiled smugly.

'It's the best pyramid I've seen,' Herbert added. Enoch floated ten feet from the ground.

Rosie sat up. 'Look you lot,' she snarled, 'Are you going to bury me or are you going to stand around all day praising that pile of bricks. I am dead you know. It's no fun lying here waiting to be buried . . . now get on with it.'

'Just a minute!' Enoch exclaimed. 'I'm not burying her in this pyramid, it's far too good for that. This is my show pyramid. Hers is over there.' Enoch pointed to an untidy heap of broken house-bricks.

Rosie sat up and followed the direction of Egyptian Enoch's pointing finger. Her eyes grew wide. She drew in a deep breath. Her mouth dropped open and her temper snapped.

'Well, of all the bloody cheek. So I'm not good enough for this one? After all, I am only the Queen of all the Negyptians. I have to be buried in a pile of mouldy bricks that's not fit for a dead dog. Well, you know what you can do with your pyramid, Enoch Thompson.' Rosie quickly stood and lashed out with her foot at the show pyramid. The bricks toppled and crashed to the ground. Suddenly Rosie realised what she had done.

'Right,' Enoch breathed through clenched teeth.

Rosie saw the danger signs and was up and running before Enoch realised it.

'I'll show her,' he hissed, and gave chase across the bombed-site. The rest of the gang watched as they disappeared towards the main road. They turned and gazed silently at the ruined pyramid.

Quietly Margaret said, 'I don't know. First the river floods, then the pyramid collapses, then the camels die, then the Queen kills herself, then another pyramid is destroyed and to finish it all, the dead Queen ends up being chased across the desert by a mad slave driver. Its been a funny old day here in Ancient Negypt.'

The gang all nodded silently.

Cast Iron Sailors

* *

THE DARNALL AQUEDUCT W.M.C Annual Children's Outing had deposited the gang in Bridlington for the day, and they were all now aboard the pleasure boat which was bucking and rolling as it made its way towards Flamborough Head.

'Oh, blow thy winter wind. Blow with all thy bloweness.' Enoch stood at the prow of the pleasure boat *Britannia* as it cut through the high waves of the North Sea. He screamed into the strong wind which moulded his holiday clothes to his cold body. 'A vast behind, Mr. Christian. U-boat off the left-hand side. Fire all sixty torpedoes. Take no prisoners.'

Rosie and Margaret huddled together in the shelter of the steering-house, rather seasick and fragile, and watched with feelings of disgust as Enoch, who seemed to have a cast-iron stomach, scooped fingers-full of winkles from a grease-proof paper bag and ate them. He turned to the girls and yelled above the banging of the waves against the rusty sides of the boat, 'It's great isn't it? You're missing all the fun.'

Rosie stuck her tongue out at him and regretted the sudden action. Her stomach bubbled in protest. Alan stumbled up the stairs from below decks and, with a staggering gait, fought his way to where Brian was dangling a piece of string with a safety pin attached into the creaming, restless, waters. 'Have you caught anything yet?' he bellowed.

'No. Not yet. But I think I had a nibble from a passing octopus a few minutes ago', Brian yelled back.

'It's great, isn't it?' Alan beamed through a wet face, 'I'm glad we came, aren't you? Where's Enoch?'

Brian nodded to where Enoch was now peering through an invisible telescope at twenty enemy destroyers, twelve submarines, and ten aircraft carriers, which he had just crippled single-handedly using a new, highly secret weapon, which only he knew how to operate from inside his trouser pocket. His hand pressed at the empty snuff tin lid again. There was a satisfying click, and another destroyer sank without trace.

From the crackly loudspeaker, which was slung to the mast of their boat, a thick Yorkshire accent announced. 'Gentlemen and ladies. The Sunny Hawaiian

Bar below decks is now open for refreshments and cheese and onion sandwiches.'
Rosie and Margaret groaned together. 'Could all passengers try not to use so
much paper in the toilet as it's blocking the bloody thing up. Thank you.'

'It's smashing to be at sea, isn't it, Enoch?' Alan yelled as he joined the one
man navy at the front of the bucking boat.

'Look!' said Enoch said in an exhilarated voice, 'There's Flamborough Head, off
the starboard port side.'

'How do you know all those sailor's words?' Alan asked.

Enoch swelled with pride. 'The sea is in my bloodness, Alan,' he replied. 'My
great grandfather worked as a fish gutter in the market.'

'Wow,' Alan exclaimed, then filling his lungs with the salty air, he felt an
overwhelming freedom at being out on the real, wet sea. Dark heavy clouds were
consolidating overhead and the waves were becoming rougher. The boat swung
out to sea to clear the shallows, and met the force head on. The accordion player
had stopped his attempts of *A Life on the Ocean Wave* and fearing a typhoon was
about to hit the boat, had scuttled below decks to seek the safety of a pint of beer
in the rolling Hawaian bar. The tarpaulin-covered passengers huddled together
in the gathering storm. As the seas built ever higher they began wedging
themselves in corners, against bolted-down deckchairs, coils of smelly ropes, in
fact anything which would hold them upright.

Only Enoch, Alan, and Brian seemed unaware of the increased motion of the
vessel. With each roll Brian's safety pin dangled clear of the water, whilst Enoch
and Alan were now signaling to their fellow smugglers on top of Flamborough
Head who watched the plight of the storm-bound pleasure boat as it fought to
turn and beat for the safety of Bridlington Harbour.

'Have a winkle, Alan.' Enoch held out the bag and offered. As Alan's fingers
closed on them, a sudden wave crashed at the boat. The bag shot from Enoch's
grasp and fell into the sea. By some miracle a winkle caught on Brian's safety pin.
A passing cod saw the gleam of pin and winkle. Brian's hands burned as the string
shot through them. It stopped abruptly as the cod's flight for freedom was
arrested by the line which was secured to the handrail.

'I've caught a fish. I've caught a fish', Brian yelled, and began pulling the taut
string back on board. Enoch and Alan slithered towards him and together they
hauled on the line. The fish threshed in the brown waves then hung protesting
as it was hauled on board. It slapped onto the heaving deck and lay with its gills
throbbing and its eyes glaring at the three.

'Flippin' 'eck', Brian gasped. 'It's massive.'

'Wow,' Alan bellowed, 'It must be three feet long.'

The helmsman had seen their performance and handing the wheel to his spotty son he left the steering house and forced his way through the lashing rain which now added to the mayhem.

'Well done,' he yelled, 'She's a good un. Here, let me put it out of it's misery.' He quickly and expertly dispatched the fish to wherever fish go in the after-life, then carrying it back to the steering house, called, 'I'll keep it safe, Son, until we reach harbour.'

All three stood bursting with pride as the other passengers muttered and nodded their heads towards them. The loudspeaker burst into crackly life once more. 'Gentlemen and ladies. Due to a sudden change in the weather I'm sorry to say we will have to cut short the pleasure trip and return to harbour. However, there is still time to enjoy a peaceful drink and sardine sandwich in the Sunny Hawaiian Bar. The captain 'as asked me to request that passengers do not attempt to use the sun deck during the return trip. Thank you.'

There was a crackle and a bang as sea spray shorted the electrical connections of the swinging speaker. It howled then faded into silence. The storm-bound holiday-makers looked at each other with fear written all over their faces. As the boat changed course the motion altered from stern to bow to port and starboard as wave after wave pushed greedily at it. Ashen faces gave way to deathly white ones, to be replaced by bright green, as the pleasure boat was transformed into a storm-torn torture chamber.

'You should never throw kitchen swill into the wind from a boat,' Enoch informed Alan in a roaring voice which carried around the boat. 'Otherwise, back it will come. Bacon fat. Tea leaves. Cold cabbage. Bits of string. The lot. Smack bang into your face.' There was a collective groan from the passengers and they rushed to the sides of the vessel.

'What are they doing?' Brian asked.

'I expect they're looking for fish. I suppose they are jealous of your catch.' Enoch answered, then continued. 'It's a dangerous profession is a sea cook's job. What with trying to make Irish stew and sago pudding at sea during a gale, a sea cook's job must be very hard.'

'Mind you,' Brian said, 'Being the captain must be a very responsible job. I mean, he's got to steer the boat and make sure the accordion player knows all the tunes that the passengers might want to hear. And he's also got to feed the ship's cat as well.'

'I thought the ship's cook fed the cat,' Alan said, 'After all, he's in charge of all the swill and things. You know. Bacon rinds and burnt beans and pork chops.' There was another collective groan from the passengers near them.

'Look,' Brian said, pointing towards the distant shore. 'What? What is it?' Enoch peered through the lashing rain.

'Look. Isn't it funny how one minute the land is up there', he said, pointing towards the fuzzy black clouds, and the next, it's down there.' He pointed to the heaving sea.

'It's the motion of the sea,' Enoch said knowledgeably, 'Up and down. Up and down. That's how it goes all the time. Up and down. Up and down. Sometimes it makes people sea-sick. I don't know why, though. It's great. It's just like being on the big dipper.'

'I expect it depends on what you've had to eat and how strong your stomach is,' Brian said. 'I mean, if you've got a stomach that's weak, well, filling it full of fish and chips and winkles and jellied eels is bound to make you feel poorly, isn't it?'

'Suppose so,' Alan answered unsurely, having consumed the aforementioned before boarding the pleasure boat. 'I must have a very strong stomach, then', Alan exclaimed with pride, 'I had all that and I feel smashing.' There was a terminal groan from the stern. From the head of the below-decks stairs appeared a navy blue jerseyed figure. He lifted a megaphone to his mouth and bellowed at the rows of backsides.

'Gentlemen and ladies. Doesn't anybody want a bloody sardine sandwich or a drink from our Sunny Hawaiian bar before we reach harbour? It's not our fault that the weather 'as turned bloody foul, you know.' He saw the hopelessness of his task and turning, shouted down the steps, 'Might as well shut the bar, Sam. This bloody lot's dying up here.'

With a disgusted look on his face he gave the prone passengers a two-fingered salute and disappeared into the bowels of the ship. Minutes later the accordion player staggered on deck wearing a crooked, beer-soaked grin. He tottered about trying to fasten the unruly instrument across his chest. After three falls to the deck and a trip over an out-stretched leg, he succeeded, and began his drunken rendition of *Boiled Beef and Carrots*. Moans and groans were caught by the wind and carried inshore. Suddenly, a blindingly bright burst of sunlight pooled the strickened boat.

'It's clearing up', Enoch cried. Then, as a fresh batch of black clouds whipped across the gap and renewed rain crashed onto the deck, he corrected, 'Oh no, it's not.'

'Look,' Alan exclaimed, 'Look. Isn't that the harbour?' They peered in the direction of Alan's pointing finger. Vaguely, through the spray and rain, they glimpsed the granite walls of the distant harbour.

'Oh, no,' Enoch groaned, 'The trip's nearly over and we've not eaten our special packed lunches yet.' He pulled a squashed bundle of damp sandwiches from under his jersey and unwrapping them, gazed at the sorry looking slices of bread and potted meat.

'Oh well, it's no good wasting good food,' and he passed the bundle around. The friends sat in the shelter of the bow and as they ate they watched with interest as first the port side passengers were high in the air and the next moment the starboard side passengers.

'They will never catch fish just leaning over the sides and looking for them,' Brian observed. 'It needs skill and a fishing line, does fishing. They must be daft. I mean, just what are they trying to do? Hypnotise them?'

The pleasure boat was now only twenty yards from the haven of the harbour and the sea calmed somewhat. The three stood, and leaning out over the bow, watched with interest as the walls loomed in front of them. People lined the safety rails and watched as the *Britannia* swung towards the harbour mouth. Enoch stood with his chest thrown out imagining they were welcoming him back from a voyage around the world. He waved his soggy sandwiches at them, pretending they were a new discovery from a distant land. When a wave was returned he thought he would faint with happiness. The boat slipped between the high walls and suddenly all was calm, and sounds of fairground rides and blaring music replaced the wild call of the sea.

The transition from the natural elements to the artificial ones of civilisation left Enoch, Brian, and Alan slightly confused. From below their feet the throb of the engines built as it reversed its screws to edge the craft up against the towering walls. Ropes fell to the deck from above, were gathered and secured, imprisoning the boat until its next trip into its natural environment.

'It was smashing, wasn't it?' Enoch beamed.

'Worth every penny,' Brian supported.

'Wish I was a sailor,' Alan added wistfully.

'Me too,' the others said, and watched with envious eyes as ropes were coiled and gangways were slid down onto the wet deck.

'I mean,' Enoch spoke, 'Every day out there on the sea catching cod and playing accordions. It must be a great life. No worries. Just piles of sardine sandwiches to scoff and jolly songs to sing.'

'And cheese and onion sandwiches,' Alan added.

'Yes, and Irish stew and sago pudding,' Brian said.

As each sea-sick passenger stumbled past them and sought the safety of *terra firma*, they glared at the trio as they stood to one side finishing the soggy sandwiches and listing sailor's fare on the rolling sea. If looks could kill, the three would have never returned from the trip and would have been posted as missing, presumed drowned, whilst scoffing food and discussing ship's swill.

Gossip

* * * * * * * * * * * * * *

'**D**OCTOR MACINTOSH says I've got to watch my foot. It could turn nasty,' Enoch's mother informed Rosie's mum. From behind the cardboard box that Enoch was endeavouring to carry homewards, a mental picture of his mother being savaged to death by her wild and wayward foot made him chuckle. Try as he might, the surreal images would not go away. He pictured his mother asleep in bed with her foot slowly and stealthily creeping up the covers to finally grasp her by the throat and, using its bunion, to throttle her. He laughed out loud. His mother stopped gossiping, turned her head slowly to him, and set her mouth in a tight-lipped, stern expression.

'I'm sure he's going barmy,' she said flatly.

'I know what you mean, love. Our Rosie's just the same,' Mrs. Bacon answered.

'Oh, before I forget. I must give him a dose of California Syrup of Figs tonight!' Mrs. Thompson exclaimed, 'That should stop him laughing all over the place. Doctor Macintosh swears by it.'

'I blame the war. The kids today get too much excitement and fun out of life. What with the bombings and all that cod liver oil and orange juice,' Mrs. Bacon said. Enoch's mother nodded vigorous agreement.

'What's wrong with your foot?' Rosie's mother enquired.

'Oh, don't ask, love. I'm a martyr to my foot. Sometimes it swells just like a balloon. And throb? It's like a drop-hammer some nights. Bang. Bang. Bang.'

'Which one is it?' Rosie's mother asked sympathetically.

'It's my left one. You know. This one.' Enoch's mother swung her leg forward for Mrs. Bacon to gaze at. Enoch noted that his mother had offered her right leg for inspection.

'Oh yes,' she breathed. 'It is swelled, isn't it?'

'Mam. That's your right foot,' Enoch said.

His mother shot him a swift, 'I'll tan your backside' look, then turning back to Mrs. Thompson, sighed and said, 'I don't know. Just what do they teach them at that school? He's just like his father. He always gets his left mixed up with his right. Enoch doesn't take after my side of the family. My mother said we were all brainy at school. I've a sister who's done right well for herself. She's an assistant secretary at the abattoir you know. Very responsible job. She counts the offal.'

Mrs. Bacon was suitably impressed.

'Mam. What's offal?' Enoch asked.

'You're too young to know,' his mother replied, then said in a half whisper, 'Don't they ask some embarrassing questions at that age?'

Rosie's mother smiled. 'I know. Our Rosie's just the same. I blame the teachers for half of it. They tell them all sorts at that school. Do you know, our Rosie even knows what frog spawn becomes.'

'Disgusting,' Enoch's mother shuddered. 'It ought never to be allowed.'

'My very words,' Mrs. Bacon replied.

'Did he give you anything for your foot?'

'An elastic bandage and some iodine.'

'Is that all? An elastic bandage and iodine?' Rosie's mother said indignantly. 'That foot of yours deserves some proper medicine. Not just iodine. It's a crutch case if ever I saw one.'

Enoch's mother basked in the sympathetic attention, then said in a self-sacrificing voice, 'I know. But there is a shortage of wood. I expect all the crutch wood went to the war effort. I'll suffer in silence. There's a lot worse off than me I expect.'

'It's a pity a lot more don't think like us. This country would be a lot better place to live in if they did,' Mrs. Bacon remarked.

Mrs. Thompson agreed.

Enoch put the box to the ground and stood awaiting his mother.

'She was in the surgery,' Enoch's mother said with a meaningful voice. 'You know. Her.'

'Oh, you mean her,' Mrs. Bacon answered, emphasising the word 'her'. 'I'm not surprised, the way she carries on. All the street knows, you know. It's common knowledge down at the welfare. Her and her carrying on. Someone ought to put a stop to it'

'Who are you talking about, Mam?' Enoch enquired.

'Nobody for nosies,' his mother answered sharply. 'Little boys should be seen and not heard. Now shut tha gob. And stop picking your nose. It'll fall off.'

'No nit nont,' Enoch replied.

'I'm sure he'll grow up daft,' Mrs. Thompson sighed.

'I know,' Mrs. Bacon agreed. 'Our Rosie's just the same. I blame them school meals. They're full of chemicals, you know. And that cook's not very clean. Her step hasn't been donkey-stoned for a week now.'

'Shocking!' Mrs. Thompson exclaimed, then scratching under her arm-pit with one hand, and easing her knicker elastic with the other, she continued talking. 'There's no excuse for it, is there? Soap and water costs nothing.'

116

Mrs. Bacon shook her head vigorously. A fine cloud of dandruff settled on her shoulders. 'I can't stand mucky folk.'

Enoch became increasingly bored as the two women continued to dissect the neighbourhood. From sheer devilment he suddenly shouted, 'Mam. Mam. My nose as nust dropped into the noad.'

His mother spun to face him in panic, saw him grinning, and raising a hand fetched him a clip around his head. 'Now be quiet, you little varmint, or I'll fetch the bobby to lock you up.'

Enoch sat on the box nursing his stinging ear. After a while he decided to take an early dinner and began eating his finger nails. Out of the corner of her eye his mother saw him. Without once breaking the flow of her gossip she interjected, 'If you carry on biting your nails you'll never play the piano when you grow up. Now stop it.'

'Our Rosie's just the same,' Mrs. Bacon said. 'At it day and night. She's got them down to her half-moons now. Mind you, I blame all these books they read. They put ideas into their heads.'

Mrs. Thompson nodded her head, causing the crocodile clips to rattle. Enoch finished his lunch and stuffed his hands in his pockets. He found two marbles and began rolling them around each other.

'Enoch,' his mother said sharply, 'Don't be disgusting. Stop it at once. It'll drop off you know. Now stop fiddling with yourself.' She turned back to Mrs. Bacon. 'Never have boys if you can help it. That's all they do. Girls are much nicer.' Then in a whisper, which had a hint of pride in it said, 'His father's just the same. Never leaves me alone. It's just as though I'm irresistible to him.'

'I know,' answered Mrs. Bacon, who wasn't going to be outdone in the marital stakes. 'Mine's the same. Mind you, I blame the potted meat. It's full of them there home-owns and half-a-dizzy-acts. It gives them wicked thoughts.'

'Mam,' Enoch begged, 'Can we go now? I'm hungry.'

'We'll go when I'm ready. Now shut up. Read your comic.'

'I haven't got a comic, mam.'

'Well, read, er, read that box you're sat on.'

'I've read it mam.'

'Well, read it again.'

Enoch knelt and began reading out loud. 'This way up. Twelve dozen Doctor Whites . . .'

His mother screamed. 'Oh my God. Enoch, don't look at that. Trust him. Of all the boxes in the shop, he has to pick that one. He'll be the death of me.'

She grabbed his arm and pulled him roughly to her side whilst Mrs. Bacon said, 'I know. Oh don't I know. Our Rosie's just the same.'

'Mam. Who's Doctor White?' Enoch asked.

His mother turned the same colour as the good doctor then flushed until she was bright red.

'He lives in another town. Now shut up.'

Enoch gazed up the street and caught sight of Alan in the distance. 'Mam, can I go and play with Alan?'

'No, you can't. You know their Brian's got chicken pox. All the family will be infested by now. I'm not having you bring foreign germs into the house.'

'But, mam,' Enoch protested, 'I've had chicken pox.'

'I don't care. You might catch them again,' his mother replied. 'Now shut up.'

'You can't catch chicken pox twice,' Enoch mumbled.

'I said shut up,' his mother menaced.

'But you can't. Teacher told us so at school.'

'See what I mean?' Mrs. Bacon exclaimed, 'That school has got a lot to answer for. They'll all end up villains when they grow up. You mark my words. Our Rosie even knows where bird's eggs come from.'

Now Enoch's mother had never pondered this question and silently wondered where bird's eggs did come from, but before she had time to probe the problem she was distracted by Rosie's mother exclaiming, 'Oh, I knew I had something to tell you! Ivy Moorhouse told me that her husband, you know her Archie, is right poorly.'

'Is he?' Enoch's mother replied, her interest stirred by memories of him having courted her back in the dim and distant past. 'What's up with him?'

Mrs. Bacon looked up the street, then down it, bent close to Enoch's mother, and whispered, 'He's got a carbuncle growing on his thingey.'

Enoch's mother looked suitably shocked. 'Never,' she breathed.

Mrs. Bacon nodded vigorously. 'He has.' Then she added, 'Mind you, from what she's told me, it's a wonder there's enough room for a pimple there, let alone a carbuncle.'

Enoch's mother knew otherwise. Her eyes grew misty as she stumbled down Memory Lane. But she replied in an innocent voice, 'He always was a frail man, though, wasn't he?'

'Ten kids is enough to make anybody frail,' Rosie's mother sniffed.

'Mam. What's a carbuncle?' Enoch asked.

Mrs. Bacon gasped, 'Oo, I'm sorry. I forgot he was there.'

'It's all right. He doesn't understand at his age,' Enoch's mother smiled.

Enoch repeated the question.

'It's a . . . a . . . a. Oh shut up, Enoch, and go and play with Alan.'

Enoch's heart leapt with joy at this unexpected freedom and without giving his mother a chance to change her mind, he sprinted off up the street towards Alan's house.

* * * *

Enoch and Alan sat on two broken, upturned buckets at the edge of the ruins and quietly watched the world going about its bewildering business.

'Well, I've never heard of no Doctor White,' Alan said. 'He can't be from around here.'

'He's got a box named after him,' Enoch said.

'Well if he's got a box named after him he must be famous,' Alan answered. 'But I've never heard him mentioned around here. He must live outside Sheffield.'

'My mother said that,' Enoch said, and sniffed. They forgot the topic as their attention was drawn to the window cleaner falling off his ladder.

'He's always doing that,' said Alan with disinterest, 'Especially in the afternoons when he's been to the pub.'

They continued to watch as the window cleaner kicked his ladder, rubbed his behind, then for good measure kicked his bucket across the street. He forgot he was wearing plimsols and fell to the floor once more as the agony of his throbbing toes gripped him.

'Waste of good water, is that,' Enoch commented.

* * * *

Mr. Moorhouse rounded the top of the street after his day at the steelworks and proceeded towards the two boys. They watched as he drew level.

'Hello, lads. How's your belly for spots?'

'Alright, Mr. Moorhouse,' they answered together.

He continued past them. Then Enoch called in a friendly way, 'Good night, Mester Moorhouse. I hope that carbuncle on your thingey finds enough room to grow alright.'

Mr. Moorhouse stood stock still. His back stiffened visibly, and they heard him hiss, 'I'll kill her when I get in. I will. I'll kill her.'